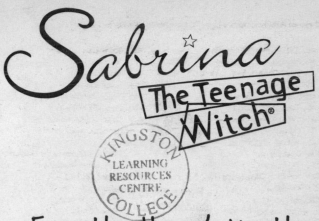

Sabrina The Teenage Witch®

From the Horse's Mouth

Diana G. Gallagher

Based upon the characters in Archie Comics

And based upon the television series
Sabrina, The Teenage Witch
Created for television by Nell Scovell
Developed for television by Jonathan Schmock

POCKET BOOKS

LONDON · SYDNEY · NEW YORK

D0610845

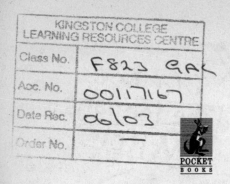

POCKET
B O O K S

An imprint of Simon & Schuster UK Ltd
Africa House, 64-78 Kingsway
London WC2B 6AH

A CIP catalogue record for this book is
available from the British Library

ISBN 0 7434 0422 X

1 3 5 7 9 10 8 6 4 2

Printed by Omnia Books Ltd, Glasgow

With affection for
Claire, Julie, and Tara Kent,
and their horses, who brighten my day from the
pasture next door.
Tally ho!

From the Horse's Mouth

Chapter 1

Sabrina eased through the coffeehouse door and paused behind several people waiting to be seated. Business was booming, which was a lucky break for her since she was trying to sneak in. Her aunt Hilda was frantically cleaning tables and not paying attention to the entrance. Sabrina bolted for the counter.

"It's about time." Josh handed a customer his change, then glanced at his watch as Sabrina dashed by. "You're late."

"I know." Upset, Sabrina ducked into the back room and slammed the door. She didn't dare talk to Josh, her aunt Hilda, or the customers until she calmed down. It wasn't their fault her adviser at John Adams College had forgotten to mention certain course requirements for her freshman year.

"Until today when it's almost too late to do anything about it!" Sabrina dropped her books and reached for an apron.

1

"What's the problem, Sabrina?" Aunt Hilda yanked open the door, leaned on the doorjamb, and folded her arms. "Besides being fifteen minutes late for your shift."

Sabrina almost snapped at her aunt, but she caught herself and took a deep breath instead. At the coffee-house, Hilda was her boss first and her aunt second. Usually their family ties didn't interfere with the business relationship, but neither of them took advantage of the situation, either.

"I can explain." Sabrina slipped the apron over her head and tied it in the back.

"You can try," Hilda said with a tight smile. She glanced back when Josh tapped her on the shoulder.

"Now would not be a good time to fire Sabrina," Josh said. "We've got them lined up to the door out here."

"Fire?" Dumbfounded, Sabrina stared at her aunt. In an emergency Sabrina expected Hilda to cut her a little slack. And flunking out of college for failure to complete one lousy course definitely qualified as an emergency. "How could you even think of firing me, Aunt Hilda?"

"Not hard when I have to pour coffee for the whole restaurant by myself because the help doesn't show up on time." Hilda's eyes narrowed. "In case you hadn't noticed, we're really busy today. The more business, the more money in tips and in the till—unless the service is so poor the customers leave, don't come back, *and* tell their friends not to bother coming in, either."

"You're absolutely right, Aunt Hilda. Losing my job isn't the worst thing that can happen." Sabrina sighed. "And it's not like *you'll* be responsible if I end up being a drain on society because I'm unemployed *and* uneducated."

"Uneducated?" Hilda hesitated, then gasped. "You dropped out of college?"

"No, but if I don't take a physical education course, Adams might drop me!" Sabrina exclaimed.

Hilda frowned, still confused. "Then why not just take a physical education course?"

"Oh, right. Like it's that easy," Sabrina huffed. "I was late because I was trying to get into one of the cool classes. I mean, Roxie could have told me she was signing up for Jazzercise *before* the class was full."

Sabrina slumped against the wall, shaking her head. Roxie was her best friend and roommate in the small, off-campus house they shared with Miles, a lovable science nerd with chronic bad hair, and Morgan, their gorgeous but completely self-centered and irresponsible resident adviser. Sabrina realized that her roommate probably didn't even know a P.E. course was required. Like the bowling class Roxie had already taken, Jazzercise was an easy credit.

"Then sign up for something else." Hilda rolled her eyes, exasperated. "I don't see the problem."

"Of course not!" Sabrina threw up her hands. "You don't have to choose between bodybuilding and high diving!"

3

"Hilda!" Josh called in a panic. "The hungry horde is getting restless!"

"And you don't have to make a decision right this minute." Hilda waved Sabrina out the door. "I'll pour coffee. You finish cleaning the tables."

"So I'm not fired?"

"Are you kidding?" Hilda laughed. "The place is packed!"

Sabrina loved working when the coffeehouse was mobbed, especially when she was in a bad mood. Aside from the extra tips, being too busy to think about anything except who ordered what flavor coffee at what table took her mind off her troubles. Making small talk with the regular customers, touching base with friends from school, and meeting new people made it hard to stay bummed.

And impossible to keep up, Sabrina thought as she wiped off a table she had just finished busing. Josh swerved to avoid running into her as he rushed by with two pieces of cheesecake for a couple on the sofa. Aunt Hilda seated two girls at a table by the front window and signaled Sabrina to take them. Nodding, Sabrina shoved her bus tub full of dirty dishes at Josh as he headed back to the counter.

"Why are you giving me this?" Josh stared at the tub Sabrina braced against his stomach.

"Because you're going toward the sink empty-handed and I've got new customers." Sabrina smiled impishly. "Better grab this tub because I'm going to let go."

"I don't think so." Matching the mischievous twinkle in Sabrina's eye, Josh held up his hands.

"On three." Grinning, Sabrina had her finger primed to point in case Josh thought she was bluffing and didn't catch the tub when she dropped it. "One, two . . ."

"Sabrina—" Josh's voice had an edge of warning, but he blinked uncertainly.

"Three!" Sabrina pulled her hands away.

"Look out!" Josh dropped to one knee and caught the plastic bin full of clanking cups, plates, and silverware. The people at the nearest tables applauded when he stood up. Flustered, he took an awkward bow.

"And now for our next trick—" Sabrina quipped.

"Forget it!" Josh fled toward the counter with the bus tub.

Chuckling to herself, Sabrina pulled her order pad out of her apron pocket when she got to the window table. Both girls were staring out the window. "Sorry about the delay. What can I get you?"

"Maybe nothing." Clearly annoyed, the blond girl turned to glare. "I don't like being ignored or kept waiting, and we were just about ready to leave."

Don't let me stop you, Sabrina thought. She started to gesture toward the door, then hesitated when she recognized Debra Sheridan. With shining, shoulder-length, platinum hair, emerald green eyes, and a flawless complexion, Debra was a classic beauty from a very old, very wealthy Boston family. Antagonizing the girl wouldn't be good for Aunt Hilda's business or Sabrina's social standing on campus.

"Are you having a bad day, too, Debra?" Sabrina asked, hoping she looked more sincerely concerned than she felt. "Boy, can I relate. I've been bummed ever since I found out we have to take some kind of physical education course. I mean, I thought I left sweat socks and stinky gym towels behind when I graduated from high school."

"Do I know you?" Debra's nose twitched slightly, as though she'd just caught a whiff of a foul odor.

The freckle-faced girl with short, curly red hair sitting across from Debra lowered her gaze to study her manicured nails.

"Not exactly." Sabrina extended her hand. "Sabrina Spellman. We're in the same English lit class."

"I'll have a café almond crème." Ignoring Sabrina's hand, Debra smiled at her friend. "What do you want, Cindy?"

Reddening, Sabrina pulled back her hand. Debra's blatant rejection and the implied contempt were intentional, but Sabrina didn't lose her temper. Trading insults with the popular socialite wouldn't accomplish anything except to give the coffeehouse a bad rep. Debra Sheridan didn't deserve any consideration, but Aunt Hilda did.

"Hot chocolate." Cindy cast a quick smile at Sabrina. She was obviously embarrassed by Debra's obnoxious behavior. "And a glazed doughnut, please."

"Sure." As Sabrina left the table, she couldn't help but overhear Debra's snide remarks.

"You didn't have to be so nice, Cindy," Debra said. "She's just a waitress and not a very good one, either."

Sabrina thought about casting a spell. A frog in her throat or purple streaks in her hair might make Debra think twice about her superior attitude. She didn't have the right to make other people feel like dirt just because she was beautiful, popular, and rich. Debra might realize that if she spent a day being ridiculed for having rotten teeth or sagging earlobes.

Except, Sabrina realized, she didn't want to lower herself to Debra's level by using magic to make the point. Besides, she had more important things to worry about.

Was staying in college worth the risk of belly flopping from the high-dive platform or becoming a muscle-bound teenage witch?

"Come on, Zelda," Salem pleaded. "Just one game."

"Not now, Salem." Zelda added a pinch of pulverized rhubarb root to the potion she was brewing on the labtop in the Spellman dining room.

"Pretty please?" Desperate, Salem rubbed against Zelda's leg. Life as a cat had never been all that exciting, especially since he had once been a warlock who almost conquered the world. Now that Sabrina had moved out to go to college and Hilda and Zelda were both working, his daily routine was worse than dull. It was totally boring, and he was going crazy!

"No!" Zelda snapped, then immediately softened her tone. "I'm sorry, Salem, but I don't have time to play with you right now. After I finish this batch of hare remover for Cousin Mortimer, I have to prepare my lesson plan for class tomorrow. One game of Other Realm Monopoly could take *days*."

"We don't *have* to collect two hundred miscellaneous spell ingredients every time we pass Go." Salem jumped onto the edge of the labtop and wrinkled his nose. Zelda's homemade hare remedy smelled like chicken feathers mixed with swamp water. "Why doesn't Cousin Mortimer just buy Rabbit Router over the counter?"

"Because the Other Realm Spell and Potion Administration took it off the market last year." Zelda covered her pungent potion and turned down the burner to let it simmer. "Rabbit Router didn't make the copies of multiplying hat hares vanish out of existence as advertised. They just became invisible."

"That could make for some pretty crowded top hats." Salem chuckled, amused by the image of Cousin Mortimer living in an apartment full of invisible rabbits. Zelda's magic formula would solve that problem in a hurry. When Mortimer's rabbits ate it, every one except the magician's original hat hare would run away to the woods to live happily ever after.

"Anybody here?" Sabrina called from the kitchen.

"Sabrina!" Salem's heart leaped with joy when the youngest Spellman witch peered through the dining room door. "I'm saved!"

"From what?" Sabrina gagged. "The stinky stuff Aunt Zelda's cooking on the labtop?"

"No, from weeks of horrible ennui!" Salem hung his head and sighed.

"Sorry, Salem, but I can't sympathize with a cat whose only problem is boredom." Sabrina sagged against the doorjamb.

"What's wrong, Sabrina?" Zelda asked as she slipped out of her lab coat.

"I hope it's serious," Salem hissed. "Since no one cares enough to entertain me, I'll settle for an impending calamity."

"Why don't I make some tea, and we'll talk about it." Zelda put an arm around Sabrina's shoulders and steered her back into the kitchen. "Whatever it is."

Salem scampered between the two humans and vaulted onto the counter. "Dismal discussions always go better with cookies, don't you think?"

"Don't you ever think about anything except your stomach, Salem?" Sabrina sank into a chair and dropped her chin in her hands.

"Only when I'm not bored or hungry," Salem said. "And lately I'm one or the other twenty-four seven."

Sabrina looked up sharply. "Guess it must be pretty quiet around here with everyone at school or at work."

"Or both." Zelda held up her pointing finger and looked at Sabrina. "Irish breakfast tea or something with more zing?"

"You choose," Sabrina said. "My decision-making neurons are already working overtime."

"Chocolate chip!" The cat leaned forward, his whiskers twitching with anticipation. Zelda zapped a cookie into his bowl. Salem looked at her. "Could you add a little milk to that?"

"We may have been neglecting you a little the past few weeks, Salem, but don't press your luck." Zelda set a steaming cup of spiced orange tea in front of Sabrina. "So what's this monumental decision you're struggling to make?"

Salem's ears perked up as he chewed. Now that he had shamed Zelda into satisfying his chocolate chip craving, he felt guilty for not feeling sorry for Sabrina sooner. *She looks like I feel when Hilda decides I need a flea bath*, he thought.

"I have to pick a physical education course to take by tomorrow." Sabrina shoveled three heaping spoons of sugar into her tea. Her frown deepened as she stirred.

"That's it? A deadline for gym?" Cookie crumbs dropped onto the counter when Salem's mouth fell open. "What kind of catastrophic problem is *that?*"

"A make-it-or-break-it-at-Adams-College kind." Sabrina pulled a paper out of her bag and handed it to Zelda. "The problem isn't having to take P.E., although I'm not exactly thrilled. It's *what* to take for P.E. I've highlighted everything that's still available."

Zelda's smile faded as she scanned the page. "Body-building, high diving, or wrestling? No wonder you can't make up your mind."

"What's wrong with wrestling?" Salem asked. "Those ladies on TV are making a bundle!"

"The school is dropping wrestling because *no* one signed up. Most girls aren't into contact combat." Sabrina sipped her tea. "And I just can't get excited about lifting weights or plunging off a platform into a pool of water."

Zelda brightened when she turned over the page. "What about beginning equitation?"

Sabrina blinked. "There's a P.E. course in good manners?"

"Not etiquette!" Zelda laughed. "Horseback riding. The college has an off-campus stable, and the beginning equitation course starts tomorrow afternoon."

"But horses are so big!" Sabrina exclaimed.

"Big, but exhilarating to ride." Zelda stared into space with a wistful smile. "I used to love riding to hounds with the young Queen Victoria. We never actually caught the fox, but we had fun. There's nothing more thrilling than racing across open country on a noble steed, leaping over fences and walls—"

"Or drenching the queen when your horse bumped into her horse and you *both* fell into the creek." Salem chuckled. "You were the talk of Paris for two weeks!"

Zelda scowled. "They knew about that in Paris?"

"Word travels fast when someone dunks the ruler of the British Empire and lives to laugh about it," Salem explained. "Good thing Vicki had a sense of humor."

11

"Getting thrown or trampled doesn't have much appeal, either." Sabrina shuddered. "Like I said, horses are big!"

"And people have been riding them for thousands of years," Zelda said. "Riding is safer than high diving and more refined than bodybuilding, but it's your choice."

"I have to work tomorrow afternoon," Sabrina argued.

"I'm sure Hilda can find someone to work your shifts until you finish the course," Zelda countered. "Especially since you need a P.E. credit to stay at Adams."

"And I'll be your coach!" Salem jumped onto the table. Helping Sabrina learn to ride was the perfect cure for his boredom. Going to the stables would be better than sitting around the house alone. He had seen every rerun of every television drama ever made. Some of them twice!

"You're kidding, right?" Sabrina eyed Salem with skepticism. "You're a cat!"

"I was a warlock for centuries before I became a cat," Salem reminded her. "And quite an accomplished horseman, too."

"That's true," Zelda said.

Salem held his breath while Sabrina considered her limited options. Horse barns were full of mice he could chase and sweet-smelling alfalfa to curl up in for naps. The resident nags might even have some inside info on the next Kentucky Derby winner!

"Well, since horses are closer to the ground than the high dive," Sabrina said, "I guess I'll have to enroll in the equitation class."

"Yes!" Salem whooped. "I even know a great cure for saddle sores!"

"For a coach, you don't inspire much confidence, Salem," Sabrina muttered.

Chapter 2

"Not too shabby," Salem commented from the passenger seat of Sabrina's car. He sat with his front paws on the armrest, looking out the window.

"Not shabby at all," Sabrina agreed as she drove down the narrow road leading to Adams College Stables. She had lucked out at registration that morning. The equitation class was limited to six, and she had gotten the last slot. Now that she had decided to learn to ride, she was eager to get started. She just hadn't expected the stables to be so picture perfect.

Tall shade trees and a stone wall lined both sides of the drive. The meadow beyond the wall on the right contained two white-fenced enclosures. Large jumps made of natural timbers, stone, and trimmed hedges dotted the green expanse beyond the riding rings. Several horses grazed in the pasture on the left. Dense woods stretched as far as Sabrina could see behind two barns at the end of the drive.

15

Sabrina parked between a dented, rusty pickup truck and a luxury model sedan in a shaded area set off from the barns.

"Squirrel!" Salem leaped over Sabrina's lap and hit the ground running the instant she opened the door. Before he reached the tree where the startled bushy-tailed rodent had taken refuge, he made an abrupt right turn. "Butterfly!"

Leaving the cat to harass the local wildlife, Sabrina tucked a riding helmet under her arm and headed for the barn.

She counted five girls waiting in front of the larger building. The lower half of the front wall was faced with stone, and the wooden planks above it were painted red. The trim on the large, double sliding doors and the smaller doors into the hayloft above was painted gray to match the stonework. The dirt drive curved around a large section of manicured grass graced by a large oak. Four girls sat on a stone bench that circled the tree's massive trunk. The fifth girl nervously watched the activity inside the barn through the open doorway. They all were wearing black or brown knee-high boots, tan or gray britches flared at the thighs, and bulky protective hard hats covered in black velvet. Thanks to Aunt Zelda, Sabrina was wearing the appropriate wardrobe and would fit right in with the equestrian set.

A smaller barn, also painted red and gray but with no stonework, stood thirty feet to the right of the main barn. The narrow side of the smaller building faced the long side of the main barn. Nobody sat on two park benches that were positioned under the windows on either side of the open doorway.

"Right behind you," Salem said. "This is going to be so much fun!"

"Not if you keep talking!" Sabrina warned the cat.

"Sorry." Salem lowered his voice. "I've been stuck in the house talking to myself for so long, I forgot."

Sabrina hadn't taken Salem's offer to be her riding coach seriously. She had brought him because he *had* been left home alone too much the past few months. The health department didn't allow pets in restaurants, and Adams didn't allow cats in class. Hanging out at the stable seemed like the ideal solution, especially since Salem had a habit of getting into trouble when he was bored. Aunt Zelda still hadn't paid off the debt he had incurred on an Internet auction buying spree.

Sabrina stopped near the girl standing by the open doorway and peered inside the main barn. Stalls with sliding doors ran the length of the barn on the left side. More stalls, a room full of riding equipment, a door marked Office, and a side aisle opened onto the wide central corridor from the right. Three horses stood in the center aisle, held in place by two ropes. The ropes were attached to the walls, one on each side. The other ends were clipped to metal rings on the horse halters. Three men were vigorously brushing the horses' shining coats and combing their silken tails.

The horses weren't the only things that gleamed, Sabrina noticed. Blankets were neatly folded on metal racks attached to each stall. Polished leather halters and lead shanks hung from hooks, and the cobbled stone floor had been swept clean. Even the dirt courtyard had been raked. The stable was more organized than Aunt Zelda's study!

"Well, I was right about one thing." Sabrina moved closer to a petite girl with short, stylish dark hair and pointed to the horse standing closest to the entrance. The animal's back was higher than the top of her head. "Horses are huge."

"I'm definitely having second thoughts about this riding thing," the girl said. "How are we supposed to make something that big do what *we* want?"

"I think that's what they're supposed to teach us," Sabrina quipped. "I mean, my aunt and my cat learned to ride so how hard can it be?"

"Your cat can ride?" The girl's expression shifted from worried to bewildered when she saw Salem sitting at Sabrina's feet. Then her head snapped up with sudden realization. "Oh, duh! That was a joke, right?"

"Uh—right! I only brought Salem with me because he hates being left home alone." Sabrina quickly introduced herself to cover her blunder and put the girl at ease. "I've never ridden a horse, and I get a little goofy when I'm scared to death."

"That makes two of us." The girl grinned. "Toni Shaw."

"Glad to meet you, Toni." Sabrina glanced toward the girls sitting on the stone bench. "Any idea what we're supposed to do?"

"Not a clue." Toni looked back toward the barn as three other girls walked out of the equipment room. Each of them carried a saddle and a white sheepskin pad. "Maybe they know."

"Can't hurt to ask." Hugging the wall to avoid the horses in the aisle, Sabrina cautiously moved toward the girls. Salem hugged her heels, and Toni brought up the rear.

The girls with the saddles didn't notice the newcomers until Sabrina spoke.

"Hi! Are you guys here for the beginning equitation class?" Sabrina asked.

"Hardly. I've been riding since I was five." Debra Sheridan glanced over her shoulder. Her eyes narrowed when she saw Sabrina. "What are *you* doing here?"

"Toni and I are here for the beginning equitation class." Sabrina was just as surprised and dismayed to see Debra as Debra was to see her, but she didn't let it show. She waved at Cindy and the third girl.

"Hi, Sabrina." Cindy nodded and brushed a stray red curl back under her black helmet.

The other girl smiled shyly. She was taller and thinner than Debra and Cindy and wore her long, black hair tied in a ponytail at the base of her neck.

Curious, Sabrina looked into the room where the horse equipment was kept. Several saddles, all wrapped in fitted canvas covers to keep the dust off, rested on racks along the far end wall. Bridles with shining metal bits hung from smaller racks on the adjacent wall. Framed pictures of horses jumping large fences and colorful horse show ribbons adorned the opposite wall above a shelf full of trophies. Storage cabinets were built into the wall under the shelf.

"Should Toni and I get saddles out of the equipment room, too?" Sabrina asked.

"That's the *tack* room, not an equipment room, and the saddles and bridles in there are *personal* property," Debra said. "The school horse tack is kept in the lesson barn."

"Oh." Sabrina wasn't sure what Debra meant, since the whole stable belonged to the school. She gestured toward the horse in the middle of the aisle. It was a reddish brown color with a striking white spot on its forehead. "Isn't this a school horse?"

"Not!" Debra gasped. "Golden Wings is *my* horse. My father *pays* to keep her here just like Cindy and Veronica board their horses, Moon Shadow and Crazy Quilt."

"I'm ready for Goldie's saddle." A second man finished cleaning dirt out of the horse's hooves, stuffed the metal pick in his pocket, and took the saddle from Debra.

"Remember not to tighten the girth until she's outside, Johnny." Debra scratched Goldie's chin.

Sabrina noted that Debra used the same condescending tone with the stable hand that she had at the coffeehouse the day before. *Does Debra think everyone who works a service job is inferior?* Sabrina wondered.

A slim, gray-haired man with a handsomely rugged face stepped out of an office door at the far end of the barn. He was wearing britches and boots, too, but with a tweed jacket over a white, open-neck shirt.

"Come into the office before you mount up, girls." The man's intense gaze flicked past Sabrina and Toni as though they weren't there. There was no question he was speaking to Debra, Cindy, and Veronica. "We need to discuss your entries in the Westbridge Hunt Club Horse Show."

"Who's that?" Toni asked when the man disappeared back inside the office. "He's kind of cute for an old guy."

"Edward Monroe," Cindy said.

"The best trainer in Boston," Veronica added.

"Great! If we're going to learn to ride, we might as well learn from the best." Sabrina nodded with approval, hoping she could break through the social barriers Debra had set up. *Maybe she doesn't realize she acts and sounds like a complete jerk!* Sabrina cast a sweeping glance at the three stable workers. "These guys are kind of handy to have around, too."

"Those *guys* are grooms," Debra explained, "but they only work with the show horses. And Edward only trains experienced riders who *own* their horses and compete. Now if you'll excuse us—" Rolling her eyes, Debra waved Cindy and Veronica to go ahead of her into the office.

Cindy looked back with an apologetic shrug.

Sabrina smiled tightly.

"Why do I have the feeling that we've just been insulted?" Toni asked.

"Because we've just been insulted," Sabrina answered.

Looking toward the office, Salem arched his back and hissed. Debra's haughty demeanor annoyed him, too.

"Smart cat," Toni observed.

"You have no idea," Sabrina said. She quickly changed the subject before Salem decided to demonstrate his higher-than-average feline intelligence. "Guess we'd better go check out the school horse barn."

Toni paused uncertainly when they left the barn. "If Mr. Monroe isn't going to teach us to ride, who is?"

"Maybe that really cute *young* guy over there." Sabrina pointed toward the smaller barn. The other four girls were gathered around a man wearing jeans and a casual, short-sleeve shirt. Average in height and build with a mop of wavy dark hair, he was calling out names and marking them off a clipboard.

"Well, we may not own horses," Toni quipped, "but we're certainly getting a better deal in riding instructors."

"Even if he's not the best in Boston," Sabrina said as she and Toni jogged toward the group.

The young man greeted them with a smile. He glanced at the clipboard, then back at the late arrivals with probing brown eyes. "You must be Sabrina Spellman—"

"That's me." Sabrina held up her hand.

"And Toni Shaw," Toni said with a curt salute.

"Okay." He checked off their names and cocked an eyebrow when Salem pounced on a grasshopper. "Is the cat with you?"

Sabrina nodded. "I hope that's all right. Salem isn't

any trouble, as long as you don't turn him loose on the Internet with a credit card."

"My folks have the same problem with my younger sister." The girl wearing glasses giggled at the shared joke and held out her hand. "Carol."

"Beth, Dixie, and Gretchen." The man pointed to the other three girls as he introduced them.

Sabrina made a quick mental association to help her remember everyone's name. Carol wore glasses and giggled. Beth chewed gum, and Dixie had long, bright red nails. Gretchen was tall and thin like Veronica, but she had short honey-blond hair.

"And I'm Mike Santori, your riding instructor." Mike's gaze lingered on Sabrina for a moment. A slight frown furrowed his tanned forehead as he lowered his eyes to jot another notation on the clipboard.

"Sorry we're late," Sabrina said. Between her delayed arrival and bringing a cat she was sure she had made a terrible first impression on the instructor. "We went to the wrong barn."

"A mistake that Debra Sheridan was quick to correct," Toni explained, sighing.

"No doubt." A fleeting look of disgust crossed Mike's face when he saw Johnny and the other two grooms lead Goldie, Moon Shadow, and Crazy Quilt out of the main barn. The three men walked the horses in a large circle while they waited for Debra and her friends.

Mike didn't seem to care much for Debra's superior attitude, either, Sabrina realized. However, she put the silly debutante out of her mind when the young instructor gave her a dazzling smile. She was suddenly glad, and a little guilty, Harvey didn't go to Adams.

"Now that everyone's here, let the course begin. This way, ladies." Mike hung the clipboard on a hook by the door as he led the girls inside.

The school horse barn was designed much like the large barn without the office. Stalls lined the left side of the central aisle, and the feed and tack rooms opened onto the aisle from the right. The remainder of the right side served as storage for a tractor, various tractor attachments, and bales of hay stacked to the roof. Although everything was clean and organized, the blankets, saddles, bridles, brushes, and other school horse gear looked used and worn compared to the equipment in the main barn.

Horsey hand-me-downs, Sabrina concluded as Mike brought the group to a halt in the middle of the barn. It was very apparent that the division between the privileged and the ordinary in the equestrian world did not just apply to people. The horses in the school barn stalls looked clean and well fed, but their coats didn't have the same quality shine as the show horses.

The horse in the stall behind Sabrina snorted. Chocolate brown with a wide, white blaze down his face, he tossed his head when she turned and caught his eye.

"Hi, horse." Sabrina placed her palm against the vertical bars that formed the top of the sliding stall door. The horse pressed his velvety nose against her skin, then curled his lip, snorted again, and turned away. "What's his problem?"

"I wish I knew." Mike shrugged. "He's been kind of cranky lately."

"Getting the brush-off from a horse won't affect my grade, will it?" Sabrina teased.

"No." Mike's amused expression became serious as he scanned the whole group. "This is a pass or fail course that doesn't depend so much on how well you learn to ride, but how well you handle the complete horse experience."

"Could you be more specific?" Sabrina asked.

"Sure. Although riding is a big part of this class, you're going to learn about the care and feeding of horses, too." Mike reached into the feed room, pulled out a pitchfork, and handed it to Sabrina. "Starting with the basics."

"You're kidding, right?" Sabrina stared at the pitchfork. He didn't really expect her and the other girls to clean the horse stalls, did he?

"Aunt Zelda!" Sabrina threw open the front door and stormed into her aunts' house. She almost tripped over Salem when he shot into the foyer ahead of her.

"Lighten up, Sabrina." The cat leaped onto the library table behind the sofa. "It wasn't *that* bad."

"How would you know, Salem?" Sabrina's eyes flashed as she stomped by. "You spent the afternoon stalking mice."

"Yeah, but I didn't catch any." Salem sprawled

across the tabletop with a sigh. "I'm failing barn cat one-o-one."

"Which may be a step up from *passing* beginning equitation." Although she had taken a shower and changed into clean clothes, Sabrina was certain she still smelled like horse manure. "Aunt Zelda!"

"Zelda!" Hilda popped into the living room. With her coffee-stained apron, chocolate-smudged nose, and disheveled hair, she reminded Sabrina of a restaurant refugee fleeing the horrors of the dinner rush.

"Sorry, Aunt Hilda, but I've got first yelling rights." Sabrina fell onto the couch and crossed her arms. "Aunt Zelda!"

"What's going on?" Zelda raced in from the study. "Is the house on fire?"

Sabrina and Hilda both started talking at once.

"I've got calluses from shoveling and brushing!" Sabrina threw up her hands. "You didn't tell me horseback riding had a major downside, Aunt Zelda."

"The coffeehouse is mobbed, and I'm losing my mind!" Panic-stricken, Hilda waved a handful of order checks. "I can't remember if the double mocha cappuccino goes to the bald guy on the sofa or the laughing lady by the door!"

"I ache all over, and I didn't even get on a horse!"

"I think I gave my last customer change for a twenty instead of a ten!" Hilda squealed. "If that keeps up, I'll be broke by the end of the week!"

"Time!" Zelda whistled for silence, then fixed Sabrina with a pointed stare. "I take it your first day at the stables didn't go very well."

"Yes. No. That depends. I mean, it wasn't exactly a disaster," Sabrina admitted. "I just didn't expect horses to be so much work."

Lesson number one had covered mucking out stalls, proper horse grooming, and tacking up, which was stable talk for putting saddles and bridles on the horses. Even though they hadn't actually ridden and every muscle in her body was sore, she had learned a lot. She also liked Mike, Toni, and the other girls. Suddenly, her complaints seemed pretty petty.

"When things are too easy," Zelda said, "there's no pride of accomplishment."

"That doesn't seem to bother Debra Sheridan much," Sabrina muttered.

While Mike had been teaching the beginning equitation class the finer points of bits and buckles, Debra, Cindy, and Veronica had trained in the ring with Edward. When they were finished, the grooms had taken care of their horses while they relaxed in the office with a cold soda. Before-and-after riding chores were not part of their horse agenda.

"Is it my turn now?" Hilda asked. "My nervous breakdown is making Josh a nervous wreck. It's hard to maintain employee confidence when the boss is falling apart."

Sabrina stiffened with surprise when Hilda's arms and legs separated from her body.

Salem blinked. "Isn't a level-five anxiety attack a little difficult to explain to your customers?"

27

"I popped out *before* I went to pieces." Hilda's disconnected arms flapped in frustration.

"Coming unglued won't solve anything, Hilda." Zelda patted her sister's back to calm her. "You've got to pull yourself together."

"I'll try." Hilda breathed in deeply and counted to ten. Her arms and legs immediately snapped back into place.

"You should be thrilled the coffeehouse is so popular, Hilda," Zelda said. "Busy means cash."

"Unless you don't have enough help." Hilda grabbed Zelda's arms. "Roxie is too busy to fill in while Sabrina's taking the riding class. I need you, Zelda."

Zelda looked shocked. "I'm a college professor, not a waitress!"

"There are worse fates, Aunt Zelda." Sabrina sighed. "At least you won't have to ride a cranky horse called Mission Impossible."

Chapter 3

"That's too tight!" Salem hissed through clenched teeth. He was lounging in the corner feed bin, hidden from view inside the stall, watching Sabrina tack up Mission Impossible.

Out of sight and *out of hearing, I hope,* Sabrina thought as she loosened the leather strap that went behind the horse's ears and buckled under his throat. So far, her second day at Adams College Stables was a vast improvement over the first. She had managed to avoid Debra, and the beginning equitation class was getting ready to ride.

When she finished the adjustment, Sabrina leaned toward the cat and whispered, "How's that?"

"Would you want to run around in circles with a leather strap choking off your air?" Salem asked. "Let it out another notch."

"I can do without the sarcasm." Sabrina scowled at the cat, but she let the throatlatch out another notch. The ex-warlock turned feline really did know about horses. Although Mike had demonstrated the procedures for grooming and tacking up a horse again, Salem's expertise had saved her from having to ask the instructor for help. So far, "the complete horse experience" wasn't as hard or as much work as she had anticipated.

Sabrina nodded with satisfaction as she studied the results of her efforts. As Salem had pointed out, the school horses had not had full-body buzz cuts like the show horses, which was one reason why their coats didn't have the same lustrous gleam. Still, some intense brushing had brightened Mission Impossible's chocolate brown coat to a respectable shine. She had even gotten most of the tangles out of his tail.

"And you're absolutely positive all this tack is on right?" Sabrina asked the cat.

The rounded front part of the saddle was over the little, bony hump at the base of the horse's neck called the withers. The girth that held the saddle in place was tight, and all the bridle buckles were fastened with their ends tucked into leather keepers so they wouldn't flap. She draped the braided leather reins around Mission Impossible's neck and clasped them under his chin as Mike had instructed.

Like I could stop two thousand pounds of horse if he decided to leave, Sabrina thought nervously. She didn't think there was much chance Mission Impossible would try to run away, though. He had stood as still as a statue the whole time she had fussed over him.

"Looks good to go to me." Salem stood up and stretched.

Mission Impossible flicked an ear and swished his tail.

"What's he doing?" Sabrina tensed and took a step back from the huge animal.

"Considering that this horse hasn't moved a muscle since we got here," Salem muttered, "it's nice to know he's not in a coma."

Sabrina liked it better when the horse didn't move. Apparently, it was not standard practice to groom and tack up horses in their stalls. However, there were only three sets of crossties in the center aisle and six horses to get ready for the same class. Mike had assured Toni, Gretchen, and Sabrina that their assigned mounts would be perfectly safe in close quarters.

When Mission Impossible continued to doze, Sabrina relaxed and wondered how Toni was getting along with Cameo, a pretty, palomino mare. She couldn't see Toni through the solid walls that formed the sides of the stall, but she had a clear view of the aisle through the bars on the sliding stall door.

Clutching a bridle, Carol dangled a metal bit in front of a very big brown gelding with a black mane and tail. "C'mon, Pepper. Open up. I am *not* sticking my thumb in your mouth!"

Mike hurried over to assist the timid girl. He didn't make a big deal out of Carol's failure to bridle the horse herself, making more points with Sabrina. He was good-looking, cool, *and* kind, an irresistible combination of character traits.

"Is everyone ready?" Mike asked when Carol finished buckling Pepper's bridle.

"I guess," Toni said from the stall to Sabrina's left. "But only because I need my P.E. credit."

"Me, too!" Beth popped her gum. "I wouldn't be here if I knew how to swim."

"I took a pass on high diving, too." Catching Mike's eye, Sabrina quickly qualified her remark. "Because I just love horses."

Mike smiled, then turned his attention back to Carol.

"Liar," Salem mumbled.

"Am not," Sabrina protested softly, patting Mission Impossible's neck. "I love *this* horse."

"Okay, ladies! Everybody out of the barn!" Mike's order was issued in a joking tone that underscored his easygoing manner and style. He had made it clear from the start that, although horses had to be handled with serious caution, there was no reason the girls couldn't have a good time, too.

"Walk to the left of your horse's head, single file," Mike said, motioning Carol to lead Pepper toward the doorway. "Give the horse in front of you plenty of room. We'll mount up after everyone's outside."

Sabrina waited until the other five horses had passed the stall before she opened the stall door. "All right, boy. That's our cue to boogie."

Mission Impossible was standing directly in front of the door, but he didn't move when Sabrina pushed on his neck to get him going.

"Come on, horse," Sabrina pleaded. She tried putting all her weight against his shoulder, but he still wouldn't budge.

"And you love *this* horse because his only speed is stop?" Salem asked.

"Very funny." Annoyed, Sabrina stepped in front of the horse. She thought about motivating the obstinate horse with a quick point, then changed her mind. The other student riders had gotten their horses to move without magic. Besides, she wasn't going to let an animal get the best of her.

Setting her jaw, Sabrina put a hand on each rein by the bit and tugged. "That's a good horse. Let's go. Don't you want to go outside and play with your friends?"

The horse planted his feet.

"Try bribery," Salem suggested. "It always works with me."

"Good idea." Sabrina dug in her heels and pulled harder, grunting with the strain. "What's it going to take? Sugar? Carrots?"

Mission Impossible threw up his head and took two steps backward, yanking Sabrina into the stall.

"Having a problem?" Mike asked, coming up behind her.

"No. He's just a little shy," Sabrina shrugged. Her cheeks burned with a warm flush. No riding mistake could possibly be more humiliating than not being able to get the stupid horse out of the stupid barn. "Convincing this horse to leave his stall is the impossible mission, right?"

Mike hesitated, then sighed. "Actually, yes."

"I was kidding," Sabrina said.

"Unfortunately, I'm not." Mike leaned against the stall, his expression distressed. "Mission Impossible has got to be the most stubborn horse I've ever met. Sometimes he's willing to work, and sometimes he isn't. Lately, he mostly isn't."

Sabrina eyed the horse with new resolve. Since Mission Impossible wasn't playing fair and doing what he was supposed to do, she didn't have to play fair, either. *It's time for a little magic,* she thought, smiling. "Well, I can be pretty stubborn, too, Mike. Give me a few more minutes."

"You've got it, but don't worry if it's a no-go." Mike looked back over his shoulder. The other girls were walking their horses around the drive, waiting. "Today's lesson won't go beyond getting on and off and steering."

"Sounds like a lesson I don't want to miss," Sabrina said.

"You won't have any trouble catching up, I'm sure. I'll see what I can do about getting you a different horse tomorrow." Mike cast a glance at Mission Impossible and shook his head. "Too bad, too."

"What is?" Sabrina asked, suddenly worried.

"Edward won't keep paying to feed a horse we can't depend on," Mike explained. "If he doesn't work—"

Mike was interrupted by an urgent squeal from Dixie.

The instructor dashed out of the barn. "What's wrong?"

34

"I just ruined a nail!" Dixie stared at the blunted end of her broken red fingernail, stunned. After several seconds, she signed in resignation.

"Wearing gloves might help," Mike suggested, "but I can't guarantee that your other nine nails will survive the course."

Dixie laughed. "I'll deal. Thanks, Mike."

"Speaking of nails, mine could use a little sharpening." Salem dug his claws into the wooden wall above the feed bin and began to scratch.

Sabrina was glad Dixie's tragedy wasn't anything more traumatic than a mangled manicure. She had her own problems. *Like getting my stalled horse in gear,* she thought, raising her finger.

"Wait!" Salem yelped.

"What?" Sabrina hesitated.

"Think before you point!" Back arched and hackles raised, Salem bristled with indignation. "Maybe we should find out *why* Mission Impossible doesn't want to move before you resort to magical jump starts."

Sabrina frowned. Mike seemed convinced that the horse was just stubborn, but he could be wrong.

Mission Impossible yawned. Either he didn't understand that he was in trouble with Edward or he didn't care.

"Maybe his shoes are too tight or something," Salem added.

"Maybe." Sabrina glanced at the horse's hooves. The U-shaped metal shoes were nailed onto the hard, outer wall of the hoof, which didn't hurt. *But what if the blacksmith had accidentally driven a nail into a tender spot?*

"Let's ask him," Sabrina said, closing her eyes to compose an impromptu spell.

No more guessing why this horse is balking.
I'll know for sure as soon as he starts talking.

With a quick flick of her finger, Sabrina cast the spell.

"Cute," the horse muttered.

"Cute *and* effective." Salem grinned with perverse feline delight. "I can't wait to hear your excuse for not moving."

Mission Impossible blinked and lifted his head. "Since when do you speak Equine, cat?"

"Since never," Salem huffed. "English has been my native language for centuries. Now, thanks to Sabrina, *you* can understand and speak it, too."

"Through the wonders of modern technology?" The horse asked, sounding impressed but not particularly surprised.

"More like the wonders of good old-fashioned magic," Salem explained.

"And if your feet don't hurt," Sabrina said, "then you've got some serious explaining to do."

"My feet are fine."

"Then why won't you leave your stall?" Sabrina glared at the horse. "You made me look pretty foolish in front of the class and Mike."

36

"You take advice from a cat and you're worried about appearances?" The horse's upper lip curled back when he laughed.

"Salem isn't an ordinary cat, and nobody outside this stall *knows* he's my coach," Sabrina said, annoyed. *"Everyone* knows I couldn't get you out of the barn. Aren't you ashamed?"

"Nope." The horse yawned again.

"Not getting enough sleep because nightmares are keeping you awake?" Salem cocked his head with genuine curiosity.

"Nightmares?" Another hearty chuckle rumbled in the horse's throat. "That's a good one. I love a cat with a sense of humor."

"And I love a horse with such discerning good taste," Salem purred.

"Your mutual admiration society is touching, but I would really appreciate some answers here!" Sabrina's temper flared. "What *is* your problem, Mission Impossible?"

"First of all," the horse snorted, "my name is George."

"George," Salem repeated, nodding. "That's got an unassuming, pedestrian ring to it."

"And secondly," George continued, "I'm on strike."

"That much is obvious," Sabrina scoffed. "What, exactly, are you protesting?"

"I'm sick and tired of being a lesson horse." George stamped a front hoof for emphasis.

"What's wrong with putting in an honest day's

work?" Sabrina asked George, dismayed. Although Debra's prima donna attitude about labor was hard to take, there wasn't much she could do about it. *But I don't have to tolerate a lazy, stuck-up horse!*

"Nothing. Show horses work a *lot* harder than lesson horses." George took a step forward and sighed as he looked out the barn door.

Sabrina followed his gaze toward the smaller practice ring where Mike was conducting the first riding lesson. The other girls were mounted and walking their horses along the white fence. The activity could not be considered even remotely difficult or strenuous.

"Reverse!" Mike yelled.

"Watch." George tossed his head. "The girls are supposed to turn the horses away from the rail to change direction and then continue walking."

Although the exercise didn't sound hard, Gretchen and Dixie both had trouble. Dominic, a dark brown bay with a white blaze and four white socks, was as lanky and tall for a horse as Gretchen was for a human. He was turning in circles because Gretchen kept pulling on the inside rein.

"Ease up on your left rein, Gretchen. *Left* rein!" Mike remained calm when the blond girl confused her left and right hands. "That's better—no! Don't let go!"

Dixie's horse, a black gelding with no white markings, was demonstrating why he was called One Way Charlie. No matter how hard Dixie pulled on the right rein to change direction, Charlie was determined to keep going around the ring to the left.

"Hang on, Dixie!" After making sure Gretchen had both hands on the reins again, Mike rushed toward Dixie. "I'm coming!"

Sabrina gave Mike more high marks for patience when he calmly grabbed Charlie's bridle and instructed Dixie to nudge the horse in the right side with her boot. Miraculously, the horse pivoted and moved off, pointed in the right direction.

"No offense, Sabrina," George said, "but plodding around with beginners on my back just won't cut it anymore."

"Nobody is *born* knowing how to ride," Sabrina argued. "We *all* start out as beginners."

"I know that, and the rest of the school horses have no problem taking on the beginning equitation duty." George pointed his muzzle toward the ring. "As you can see, they take great pride in making things interesting."

Too true, Sabrina thought as Toni's palomino mare refused to pass Carol and Pepper. At least, Cameo was in the ring!

"But it's show time or no time for me from now on." A gleam of stubborn determination sparkled in George's big brown eyes.

"You can hardly blame George for wanting to move up in the world," Salem said.

"I admire your ambition and your honesty, George," Sabrina said sincerely, "but if you want to be a show horse, don't you have to get out there and *show* people what you can do?"

"Ha! Who's going to care?" George snorted with disgust. "Nobody will give me a chance because I don't have a fancy pedigree."

"That doesn't seem fair." Now that she understood George's problem, Sabrina sympathized. It was very similar to Debra's superior attitude toward working people. "Seems to me that horses should be judged on their abilities, not their family—just like people."

"Exactly. That's why I'm on strike." George backed up, shaking his head. "I may not be a registered thoroughbred, but I can walk, trot, canter, and jump just as well as those guys in the main barn."

"I've got news for you, George," Sabrina said. "If you don't start earning your keep, you may have worse problems than plodding around with a beginning rider on your back."

"Oh, yeah?" George fixed Sabrina with a skeptical eye. "Like what?"

"Well, I don't have all the details, but if you don't do what you were hired to do, I'm sure you won't get promoted. So to speak." Sabrina really didn't want to think about the possible ramifications facing a horse that wouldn't work. "So why don't we make a deal."

"I'm listening." Despite his challenging tone, George's ears flicked uncertainly.

"This should be good." Salem's ears perked forward expectantly.

"Okay." Sabrina took a deep breath. "I'll do everything I can to help you prove to Edward that you should be a show horse. In return, you'll cooperate with me so I pass this course and get my P.E. credit."

"What's the catch?" George asked suspiciously.

"No catch," Sabrina assured him. "I'll even keep the talking spell active until the course is finished. You just can't talk to anyone but Salem and me."

"Sabrina's not much of a conversationalist," Salem said, "but I'm a master of snappy patter and interesting anecdotes. Not to mention the fact that I'm up on all the stable gossip."

"Can I sleep on it and let you know tomorrow?" George asked.

"Sure." Sabrina smiled, but she wasn't as confident as she appeared. Since she couldn't use magic to influence Edward's decision against his will, she couldn't promise George that Edward would make him a show horse. All she could do was try.

And hope that George would understand if she failed.

Chapter 4

"Time to get busy, Zelda." Hilda reached into the coffeehouse storeroom and pulled her new, reluctant waitress out. "You're on the clock, and I want my money's worth."

Zelda immediately squatted behind the counter and whispered, "Has Professor Zori left, yet?"

"Two minutes ago." Hilda dumped soggy coffee grounds into the trash and put a new, white paper filter into the metal basket. "His table needs busing. Make yourself useful."

Zelda started to rise, then ducked back down when she heard the door open. "Who's that?"

"The mailman." Hilda scooped fresh coffee into the filter and looked down at Zelda as she slipped the basket into the coffeemaker. "Are you going to duck and hide every time someone you know from the college comes in?"

"If anyone from Adams recognizes me, Hilda, it

could be very embarrassing." When Zelda had agreed to take Sabrina's shifts at Hilda's Coffeehouse, she hadn't realized that she would have to serve so many colleagues and even worse, students. She wasn't sure she could keep their respect after she accidentally spilled a hot latte on them.

"But there's no point in having you here if you don't serve the customers." Hilda flipped the switch on the coffeemaker and began scooping coffee into additional filters. Having them premeasured saved time during a rush.

"Can't you call Rent-A-Server?" Zelda scanned the floor as she slowly got to her feet. The coffeehouse was empty except for two elderly women sipping tea on the sofa.

"Not!" Hilda gasped. "Those people get *twice* as much per hour as I have to pay you."

"But my academic reputation is at stake." Zelda squeezed the excess water out of a wipe rag and cleaned a streak of white icing off the doughnut case.

"And my business reputation is at stake." Hilda wrinkled her nose. "I never realized you were such a snob, Zelda."

"This has nothing to do with being a snob. I'd just rather not set a precedent pouring coffee for the head of the science department." Zelda pouted, stung by Hilda's accusation. "Besides, I've worked as a scullery maid before."

Hilda rolled her eyes. "Only because you insulted Ben Franklin and were forced to hide out in a colonial tavern for a couple of hours."

"Well, that lightning bolt *did* make his hair frizzy!" Zelda grinned, remembering back. "Who knew he was so sensitive about his appearance. Or that he wanted to take *credit* for discovering electricity," she muttered. Witches had known about electrical power long before Ben Franklin was born.

"Afternoon, Hilda!" A man wearing a business suit and carrying a briefcase walked in.

Zelda jumped and hid her face with her hand.

"The usual, Jonathan?" Hilda smiled as the customer took a table by the far wall, then she scowled at Zelda. "Relax. He sells insurance."

"Sorry." Zelda winced.

"Finish filling the coffee filters. I'll take care of Jonathan and bus the table." Rolling her eyes, Hilda stuffed the end of Zelda's wipe rag in her back pocket.

While Hilda delivered hot chocolate and an order of banana nut bread to the salesman, Zelda stacked coffee filters and fretted. Being seen working at the coffeehouse was only part of her problem. Her real problem was that she couldn't admit to Hilda that she felt overwhelmed by the whole waiting-on-tables routine.

When Hilda returned, she eyed the three-foot-high stack of nested coffee filters with obvious dismay. "Those should hold us until the end of the week."

"Is that good or bad?" Zelda asked.

"That depends on how many complaints we get because we're serving stale coffee." Hilda sighed. "It loses that fresh-roasted aroma when it's exposed to air too long."

"Oh, well, I can fix that." Zelda started to flick her finger to put half the coffee and filters back in their original containers.

"Are you nuts?" Hilda grabbed Zelda's hand. "Somebody might see you!"

"Sorry, I wasn't thinking," Zelda apologized. "Then we're stuck with too many prepped filters and stale coffee," she snapped, flustered.

Hilda reached under the counter and pulled out a roll of cellophane wrap. "Try sealing some of them in this."

"You don't have to be so smug about it." Zelda yanked the plastic wrap out of Hilda's hand, but she was more upset with herself than angry at her sister. Solving such a simple problem should have been a no-brainer for a physicist with several advanced degrees. Instead, she was so flustered she could barely function!

"I'm sorry, Hilda," Zelda said with genuine regret. Hilda and Sabrina were counting on her, and she couldn't let them down. "It's my first day, and I'm just a little disoriented."

"I don't understand why," Hilda said. "You used to wait on people all the time at the clock shop."

"I know, but I wasn't working at the college, then. And there was no danger of scalding anyone with a broken cuckoo clock." Zelda twirled the cellophane roll on its box, trying to find the loose end of the wrap. "And this job isn't as easy as I expected."

"Just because it's not rocket science, doesn't mean it's a snap." Hilda illustrated with a snap of her fingers

46

and a casual point at the box. "I'm sure you'll get the hang of it."

Zelda stared as the end of the cellophane wrap magically lifted off the roll. "What happened to the no-magic rule?"

"No magic the customers can *see*," Hilda explained with a glance around the shop. The insurance man was filling out forms, and the old ladies were whispering with their heads together. "Nobody's looking."

"Are you deliberately trying to make this more difficult for me?" Zelda frowned, hurt.

"No, you're doing a fine job all by yourself." Hilda smiled as she turned toward the door. "Oh, good. Here comes Josh. Just in time to save the afternoon business."

"Who's that with him?" Zelda squinted to peer through the front window.

"Miles!" Hilda waved as both young men bounded through the door. "Hi, guys!"

Zelda instantly spun around to face the back wall. Miles was one of Sabrina's roommates and one of her students. Well intentioned, but a little eccentric, Miles had had a crush on her for a while. Although he insisted he was over it, Zelda wasn't convinced. Her problems working at the coffeehouse were already too complex for comfort. Having to deal with the adorable but bumbling and enamored Miles, too, was more than she could handle.

"Hey, Hilda." Miles greeted Hilda with a lopsided grin and leaned on the counter. "How's it going?"

"I've had better days," Hilda said. "And worse."

"Me, too. I've got two major papers to write by next

Monday." Josh grabbed an apron from the storeroom and glanced in Zelda's direction. "Is this the new help you promised, Hilda?"

Zelda turned away, fumbling with the plastic wrap. Josh went to Emerson, not Adams, but one word to the wrong customer was all it would take to crank up the campus rumor mill. Wanting to avoid any uncomfortable situations with Miles and protect her status as an Adams College professor, she needed a plan in a hurry.

"Yes, this is—" Hilda started to introduce Zelda.

Zelda executed a quick point that added forty pounds to her slim frame. Thick glasses, protruding teeth, a larger nose, and a deeper voice completed her disguise. Adopting a loud, boisterous demeanor, she threw out her arms as she turned and bellowed, "Sabrina's cousin, Glenda!"

Everyone ducked as the roll of unraveling cellophane flew through the air. Miles caught it as it sailed over his head.

"Glenda." Hilda blinked but recovered quickly. "Luckily she could pop in to replace Sabrina."

"Oh, sorry about that!" Zelda/Glenda looked at Hilda with a sheepish shrug. "The cellophane, I mean." Then, still holding onto the free end of the plastic wrap, she worked her way over to Miles' end.

"Well, welcome to Westbridge, Glenda," Josh said with a warm smile. "We'll try to make working here as painless as possible."

"Glad to meet you, Glenda." Miles cocked his head as he handed the cellophane roll back. "Has anyone ever told you that you look a lot like your aunt Zelda?"

Zelda/Glenda stared at Miles, stunned.

"Probably not," Hilda answered, her eyes gleaming with amusement. "But I'm sure *Zelda* would love to know why you think so."

Miles studied Zelda/Glenda for a moment, rubbing his chin. "Must be the eyes."

"Now that you mention it . . ." Josh leaned toward Zelda/Glenda for a closer look, then jumped back when both her eyeballs rolled toward the bridge of her nose.

Cross-eyed Zelda/Glenda relaxed when Miles shifted self-consciously.

"Funny," Hilda said. "I don't see a family resemblance at all."

Roxie slid into the driver's seat as Sabrina slid out the door. "Thanks so much for loaning me your car, Sabrina. Are you sure you don't mind?"

Like I could refuse, Sabrina thought, grabbing her riding hat and bag from the back seat. Her roommate, who rarely displayed a degree of enthusiasm above lukewarm about anything, was almost eager as she gripped the steering wheel. Not a huge surprise considering that Roxie had procrastinated about completing a history project that was due the next day. Sabrina had agreed to be dropped off at the stables early because Roxie needed time and the car to visit as many local historical markers as possible.

"Not at all. If I can't get a ride home, I'll call." Sabrina closed the door after Salem jumped clear and waved as Roxie drove off.

"Where are you going?" Salem asked when Sabrina turned in to the main stable instead of going directly to the lesson barn.

"To use the mirror in the rest room, another amenity the school horse barn doesn't have." The staccato tap of Sabrina's boots on the stone floor reverberated through the rafters. Except for the horses in the stalls, the stable was deserted.

"Everybody must have gone out for a late lunch," Salem observed, echoing Sabrina's thoughts.

"Apparently." Sabrina paused when she reached the bathroom, which was sandwiched between the tack room and the office. "Tied back seems to be the acceptable equestrian style for long hair, but I can't decide if a bun, a ponytail, or a braid would look better under this thing." She held up her hard hat.

"George has to make the decision of a lifetime, and you're worried about your hair?" Salem sat, twitching his tail.

"Ten minutes won't make a difference to George," Sabrina countered, "but bad hair can totally ruin a girl's day. So what do you think? Braid, bun, or ponytail?"

"Braid," Salem stated without hesitation. "A bun is too formal, and a ponytail is so sixth grade."

Sabrina frowned. "Veronica wears her hair in a ponytail."

"Uh-huh." Salem nodded. "If you were on the swim team, would you shave your head like the other kids so you could swim a few hundredths of a second faster?"

"No!" Sabrina recoiled at the thought.

50

"I think I've made my point." Salem stood up to leave. "Now, if you'll excuse me, I'm going to visit George while he can still carry on a conversation. You've got to respect a horse who balks on principle."

Sabrina watched the cat saunter away, annoyed because he made so much sense. She wasn't indifferent to George's problem and hoped the horse accepted her offer, especially since she could relate. During the past couple of days, Debra Sheridan had missed no opportunity to remind her that she was not one of the equestrian elite. Sabrina usually didn't care about appearances or make decisions based on what other people thought, and she wasn't going to start now. However, Debra's taunting added an element of unpleasantness to the "complete horse experience."

"But since I'm here and I've got time, I might as well make my hair the best that it can be." Sabrina stepped into the rest room, closed the door, and flipped on the light.

A small shower stall, commode, and pedestal basin had been crammed into the tight space, and there was barely enough room to turn around. As Sabrina set down her bag and pulled out her comb, she realized the tiny room wasn't soundproof, either. She could hear every word of the conversation in the adjoining office with perfect clarity.

"I know that teaching the beginning equitation class is a burden, Michael—"

Sabrina recognized Edward's deep baritone voice.

She hadn't realized that *everyone* had a problem with the beginning riders. Of course, she was the only one who knew that George had an opinion.

"—but I simply can't handle it right now," Edward continued, "not with the Westbridge Hunt Club Horse Show only two weeks away."

"I don't mind teaching the class, Edward," Michael said. "They're a great bunch of girls, and it's actually fun."

Woohoo, Mike! Sabrina smiled as she separated her hair into three sections at the base of her neck. She should have known that Mike was too cool to be a snob.

"Hard on the nerves," Mike added, "but fun."

"I'm glad you feel that way, Michael, because—"

Sabrina tensed when Edward paused. Intuitively, she knew that bad news would follow.

"—I can't increase your pay even though you're taking on extra responsibility. There's just not enough money in the budget."

"I see." Michael hesitated. "Then maybe—"

"I'm afraid there's nothing I can do," Edward insisted. "I simply must give Debra, Cindy, Veronica, and the other students who board horses here my undivided attention. Their parents expect them to show well *and* win."

Sabrina sensed an "or else" in Edward's argument. Would the head instructor be in trouble if Debra and the other horse owners *didn't* win?

"Yes, I understand," Mike said with strained patience. "I just thought that maybe one of the other grooms could help me in the lesson barn."

"Absolutely not!" Edward sounded appalled. "I need all of them to make sure the boarders and their horses get top-notch service and care. I'm sure your students won't mind helping you with the work. There's no such thing as a free ride."

Frowning, Sabrina tied off the end of her braid. She and the other girls *didn't* mind doing the chores now that they were over their initial intimidation. However, the assumption that Mike should take on extra responsibility without extra pay or help seemed grossly unfair. She didn't like the idea that the class had to work so Debra and her friends wouldn't be inconvenienced, either, but their parents *were* paying the college to take care of their horses.

"I didn't see Mission Impossible in the ring yesterday," Edward said, changing the subject and his apologetic tone. Now he sounded annoyed. "If he's not working out, the manager at Green Hills Rental Stable will be glad to take him off our hands."

"No, that won't be necessary." Mike responded quickly, as though he hated that idea. "I'm sure the horse will be fine. I just have to figure out his quirks."

"We don't have to bother with a problem horse, Michael," Edward said. "I can get another old plug for the beginners that won't require special handling."

Old plug? Sabrina's confidence faltered as she put on her hard hat. Apparently, Edward thought George wasn't even good enough to be a good school horse! How was she going to convince the head instructor that George should be a show horse?

"It's not going to be easy," Sabrina mumbled. Her only hope of saving George was the horse's stubborn determination, *if* he accepted her offer. Considering the urgency of her mission, Sabrina shouldered her bag and popped into George's stall.

Startled by Sabrina's unannounced appearance, George whinnied with fright and jumped about six feet. He backed into a corner, shaking. "Wha-what's that?"

"Sorry. It's just me." Sabrina dropped her bag outside the stall door.

"The teenage witch who apparently doesn't care if she becomes a tabloid headline with fifteen minutes of fame that will ruin her life," Salem drawled from his perch in the feed bin.

"I'm glad to see you, Sabrina," George said, "but most people use the door."

"And most horses and cats can't talk." Sabrina exhaled, collecting her thoughts. "What do you know about Green Hills Rental Stable?" she asked George.

Mike answered as he entered the barn. "They rent horses for trail rides by the hour."

"What's so awful about that?" Sabrina turned to Mike with a bewildered frown.

George moved forward to peer at the young instructor over her shoulder.

"The animals at Green Hills are overworked and underfed," Mike explained. He reached through the bars to scratch George under his chin. "And the people that rent them usually don't know how to ride. It's a rotten life for a horse."

George snorted in agreement.

Salem's eyes narrowed. Wiser in the ways of the world than the horse, the cat realized something was wrong.

"Why do you ask?" Mike looked at Sabrina, curious.

"I, uh—was in the bathroom and overheard you talking to Edward." Sabrina shrugged an apology.

Mike nodded. "Then you know that Edward threatened to sell Mission Impossible to Green Hills if he doesn't shape up."

George gasped and threw up his head.

"It's okay, George!" Sabrina placed her hand on his neck to calm him. She felt a twinge of guilt because she had deliberately set him up to be shocked. It was the quickest, surest way to get the horse to agree to her deal and cooperate. "I won't let anything bad happen to you."

"George?" Mike put one hand on his hip and scratched his head with the other.

"It's easier to say than Mission Impossible and not nearly as negative." Sabrina shrugged. "Besides, I think he likes it."

George pushed his head under Sabrina's arm, hiding the way Salem did when he was upset, as though not being able to see would make his problems disappear.

"He certainly seems to like you, and you've got a point about his name." Mike grinned. "I just hope you can get *George* to behave."

"He will." Sabrina pulled George's head up and

looked him in the eye. "Because he doesn't want to be sold to the rental stable. Right?"

George moved his head up and down and snorted to seal the deal.

"You've really got a way with horses, Sabrina." Mike looked at George with a thoughtful frown. "It's almost as if he understands everything you say."

"I can't imagine why," Salem mumbled under his breath.

"Yeah, weird, huh?" Sabrina laughed to cover the cat's sarcastic comment and shifted topics to distract Mike. "Too bad getting you a raise won't be as easy as saving George."

"A few extra dollars would be great," Mike said. "I'm going to Adams on a scholarship, but I have to work to pay my living expenses. What little I have left over goes in the bank for veterinary school after I graduate."

Sabrina's opinion of Mike went up again because he was willing to work to get what he wanted. Her aunts had taught her that anything worth having was worth working for, a concept that hadn't been easy to accept ever since she found out she was a witch. However, magic wasn't a solution to every problem or situation. She had to go to school to learn just like everyone else. In fact, she had even had to study *magic* to get her Witch's License!

"Believe me, Sabrina, I'd be a lot happier and a lot richer if the school had hired me to be an instructor instead of a groom." Mike reached for a broom leaning against the next stall and began to sweep the aisle.

"Then Edward shouldn't expect you to do his job!" The injustice outraged Sabrina, but she tempered her anger.

"If Edward wants me to give a few lessons, I can't afford to argue." Mike opened Pepper's stall and swept a small pile of loose bedding inside. "I need this job."

"I'm glad you're teaching our class, Mike," Sabrina said, "but there's got to be some way to convince the school to pay you for doing it."

"Not likely. Having riders from Adams win horse show ribbons is a bigger priority than beginning equitation." Mike looked up from his sweeping, rolling his eyes. "There's no *prestige* associated with teaching a few students to walk, trot, and canter a horse around in circles."

Sabrina was instantly struck with an idea that was so brilliant, she couldn't believe a magical "bright idea" lightbulb had not flashed on above her head. If it worked, it would fix George's identity crisis *and* solve Mike's extra-pay-for-extra-work problem.

"I bet there would be a lot of prestige associated with a beginning equitation student winning a ribbon at the Westbridge Hunt Club Horse Show in two weeks." Sabrina smiled, suddenly excited by the prospect of competing to help George and Mike.

"Probably." Mike nodded, numb for a moment. Then he burst out laughing. "But that's not going to happen."

"Oh, I don't know." Sabrina cast a satisfied smile at

George as Mike swept his way out the door. "I think we can handle it, don't you, George?"

"Sure we can, Sabrina." George nuzzled her ear.

"No problem!" Salem exclaimed. "Except one."

"What's that?" Sabrina asked.

The cat sighed, mocking her ignorance of the obvious. "You don't know how to ride!"

Chapter 5

"**N**eed help getting George out of his stall, Sabrina?" Mike paused by the door as the other horses and riders filed past.

"Nope." Sabrina smiled tightly. "We'll be out in a minute."

"Okay." Mike glanced at the horse as though he didn't expect him to cooperate, then left shaking his head. "Holler if you need me."

Sabrina waited until everyone was out of the barn, then sagged against the stall.

"What are we waiting for?" George asked in a whisper.

Salem ran a damp paw over his right ear and paused before giving it another lick. "If I were a betting cat, which I am, I'd put my money on an instant riding spell."

"Except everyone thinks I'm a beginner." Sabrina fastened the leather chin strap on her helmet and took a deep breath. "I *don't* know how to ride, and a spell could backfire."

59

"Do we have a problem?" George's ears twitched with worry.

"Not if Sabrina uses a progressive ability spell," the cat said.

"Aren't they illegal?" Sabrina frowned. The sudden appearance of the Other Realm Rule Bearer, a short lady dressed in court styles that were centuries out of date who stood on a stool reciting the text of broken magic rules, would be a little hard to explain to the casual observer.

"Not if you need the ability to help someone other than yourself," Salem explained. "George, in this case."

"But I'm taking this class because *I* need the P.E. credit." As Sabrina had learned over the years, a lot of spells, especially ones that made life easier, had unintended consequences. There was always a downside if magic was used for personal gain. "The whole point of the class is to *learn* to ride."

"Except that this is a pass or fail course, and all you have to do to pass and get credit is *show up*." Salem chuckled. "I love it when I figure out how to beat the system."

Sabrina couldn't fault the cat's logic. Not even Other Realm bureaucrats could find and fill in every loophole in hundreds of rules.

"Trust me," Salem added with a sly grin. *"How* you learn how to ride is irrelevant under these specific circumstances."

Trusting an ex-warlock turned cat whose devious nature often resulted in Salem's outsmarting himself didn't dispel Sabrina's misgivings, but she didn't have any other options.

"Only because George and Mike's futures are at stake," Sabrina said, closing her eyes. A spell so she would learn fast, but not too fast, had to be worded just right. When she had what she hoped was an appropriate rhyme, she took another deep breath and began to chant.

> *Slow and steady riding progress,*
> *Two weeks to learn, no more, no less;*
> *Step by step so none can spot it.*
> *Show me once, by Jove, I've got it.*

A shower of golden sparkles enveloped Sabrina as she flicked her finger to initiate the spell.

"The rhyme was a little lame, but you get an A for dazzling. Now if you'll excuse me, I'll go find a comfortable spot so I can nap, I mean coach, without being conspicuous." Salem jumped to the top of the front stall wall, then chuckled again as he dropped to the floor and ran out the door. "It's show time!"

"Why is Salem laughing?" George asked as he followed Sabrina out of his stall.

"I'm afraid to ask, but don't worry. We're on a roll." Sabrina grinned as she led the horse into the bright afternoon sun. "We made it out of the barn."

"I'm thrilled." George turned to regard Sabrina with a wary eye when she stopped in the middle of the drive.

Sabrina ignored the horse's droll sarcasm and focused on the saddle. "Now if I can just figure out how to get on." Copying the other students, she pulled the stirrups down to the end of the narrow leathers, then tried to mount on George's left side. However, she couldn't quite lift her leg high enough to insert her boot in the metal stirrup.

Okay, so why isn't my ability spell kicking in? Sabrina wondered as she grabbed the front and back of the saddle to pull herself off the ground. *Because I goofed when I cast the spell! I won't know anything until somebody* shows *me once!* Stricken when she realized her mistake, she lost her grip and landed on her backside on the ground.

"Not exactly a picture of grace, Sabrina," George complained, muttering.

"You're not helping," Sabrina whispered back.

"I'm standing still!" George huffed. "How much help do you need?"

"Shh!" Sabrina stood up and dusted off the seat of her britches. A flush of humiliation warmed her cheeks when she saw Debra watching from the entrance into the main barn.

"Why don't you try using the mounting block, Sabrina?"

Sabrina's botched attempt to mount had bruised her pride. Having Debra as a witness just made it worse. Shaking her head, Debra led her mount to a wooden box with two steps by the corner of the stable.

Debra cast a gloating, sidelong glance at Sabrina as she placed her foot in her stirrup. She swung onto

Goldie's saddle in a single fluid motion. Gathering the reins, she urged the chestnut mare into a walk and headed toward the large ring on the crest of the meadow.

"Oh, no! It's Goldie." Upset, George cringed and hung his head.

"Tell me about it," Sabrina mumbled.

"Why didn't you tell me about the mounting block, George?" Sabrina asked when Debra was out of earshot.

"I'm a horse, not an instruction manual." George pouted, planting his feet when Sabrina tugged on the reins. "Why didn't *you* tell me to expect some embarrassing moments?"

"Making a fool of myself wasn't part of the plan!" Sabrina matched the horse's indignation.

"Like that matters?" George glared at her. "What kind of learn-to-ride spell did you use anyway? You fell *off* before you even got *on!* In front of Golden Wings, the most beautiful mare in the barn!"

George's plaintive tone gave Sabrina pause. "So?"

"So any hope that Goldie might *finally* decide to talk to me—a lowly school horse—is gone now!" George tossed his head.

Sabrina suddenly understood why George was being so difficult. He liked Goldie, who was, apparently, as stuck-up as Debra. Trying to get the conceited mare's attention probably had a lot to do with George's desire to be a show horse, which was a plus for her, Sabrina realized. She could use the cranky horse's crush to her advantage.

"There's only one way to impress Goldie, George," Sabrina said. "Win a ribbon at the horse show."

"With you riding me?" George sighed with profound misery. "It's hopeless!"

"Don't you think you should give me the same chance to prove myself that you want Edward to give you?" Sabrina crossed her arms, defying the horse to refuse.

"I suppose so," George admitted grudgingly. "Come on, then. We're wasting time."

George trotted up to the mounting block leaving a billowing cloud of dust and a determined teenage witch in his wake.

"You won't regret this, Sabrina." Salem peeked out the leather flap as Sabrina switched the saddlebags to her other shoulder.

"I already do. You're heavy." Sabrina shoved Salem's head down as she approached Hilda's Coffeehouse. Although cats weren't allowed in the restaurant, they were both starving and he had promised to keep a low profile. Besides, she couldn't stand listening to the cat's pathetic sobs.

After the lesson, Sabrina and Toni had stayed to help Mike clean up and feed. Since no one else was available to give her a ride, she and Salem had cruised Westbridge with Toni while she ran some errands. Toni lived on a strict budget and chose her routes to conserve gas. Sabrina appreciated the ride, but when the perky dark-haired girl stopped to do laundry, she had decided to

walk the rest of the way home—after a quick detour to
the coffeehouse to chow down.

"Food!" Salem moaned. "Does Hilda stock *anything*
made of fish?"

"Shh!" Sabrina smiled innocently when a passing
gentleman looked at her oddly.

"So it's okay for the horse to talk but not the cat?"
Salem emphasized his final words by slamming back
down into the saddlebag. A muffled "Ow" followed,
and then, thankfully, silence.

*What would she do about George? A lovesick horse
with a sarcastic streak, an ambitious agenda, and a rotten suspension system,* Sabrina thought, wincing as she
pushed through the coffeehouse door. She ached all
over, an ailment she hoped her aunts could cure since
Salem's saddle sore remedy didn't work on tortured
muscles. At least she had a psychological handle on
George now, which made the physical problems a little
easier to bear.

"What a surprise!" A heavyset woman with large,
prominent teeth and thick glasses smothered Sabrina
with a hug.

Sabrina grunted as massive arms crushed her against
a dark green coffeehouse apron. In danger of blacking
out from lack of oxygen, she gasped, "I can't breathe!"

"Oh, sorry." The blond woman immediately let go
and stepped back with a chagrined expression.

"What happened to 'please, wait to be seated' or 'I'll
be right with you'?" Sabrina asked as she stumbled to
the nearest chair. She sat down with a groan and placed

the saddlebags on the floor. "I know the standard welcoming phrases are boring and insincere, but they don't put the customers' ribs at risk."

"Hi, Sabrina!" Aunt Hilda waved from the counter as she finished making change for the last customer. She followed the man to the door to lock it behind him.

"You don't know who I am, do you?" The new waitress nibbled her lower lip in nervous expectation of Sabrina's response.

"Who is this?" Sabrina asked Aunt Hilda. Apparently, Aunt Zelda had decided *not* to fill in at the coffeehouse as her replacement.

"Here's a hint," Hilda said, flipping the Closed sign so it faced the street. "It's *not* Cousin Glenda."

"We don't *have* a Cousin Glenda," Salem muttered, popping his head out of the saddlebag.

"What's he doing here?" The new waitress frowned.

"Looking for a handout." The cat chirped with dismay as he eyed the woman up and down. "My, my, Zelda. I never knew working in a coffeehouse could be hazardous to your physical attributes."

"Aunt Zelda?" Sabrina's mouth fell open. On closer inspection, she could vaguely identify her pretty aunt under the homely disguise.

"Cousin *Glenda*," Aunt Zelda corrected. Buried in the puffy face, her eyes looked small and beady when they narrowed in warning.

"Don't ask." Hilda rolled her eyes as she hurried back to the cash register to begin tallying the day's receipts.

"I won't," Sabrina said, taking the hint. She didn't

need to know why her attractive Aunt Zelda was parading around the coffeehouse as a dumpy, middle-aged matron. "Could I just have a hot mint tea and two jelly doughnuts?"

"Copy that." Salem slipped out of the leather bag and hopped onto the chair beside Sabrina. "Except substitute milk for the tea and Bavarian Crème for the jelly."

"And if anyone asks," Sabrina added when Zelda/Glenda's frown deepened, "there's no cat here. He threatened to report me to the Be Kind to Familiars Who Used to Be Warlocks Society because I put in some overtime at the stables and he missed dinner."

"There aren't any mice in that barn?" Zelda/Glenda asked.

"Could you eat someone who's cute and furry with big brown eyes and who doesn't mind an occasional round of cat-chases-mouse just so you won't be bored out of your mind?" Salem crossed his front paws on the table and cocked his head. "Hmmm?"

"Couldn't catch any, could ya?" Hilda stated more than asked. "So how did your riding lesson go today?"

Sabrina paused, unsure how to begin her report. Getting aboard George had been easy using the mounting block, but the lesson hadn't been the slam dunk she'd expected.

"Well, I finally rode the horse," Sabrina said.

"If by riding you mean that she got on and learned to steer," Salem scoffed.

"When the lesson was over, I could keep my heels down, my elbows in, and I wasn't hanging onto the front of the saddle for dear life," Sabrina added defensively. "Mike said my posture was perfect, after I stopped slouching."

"If *my* future depended on that rate of progress, I wouldn't be sleeping nights." The cat gave Sabrina a pointed look.

Sabrina understood that Salem was concerned about George, but she didn't want to tell her aunts that she had used a spell, even if it was to help George more than her. She knew they wouldn't approve no matter what she said were her intentions. Besides, it wasn't working the way she'd hoped. Instead of automatically knowing how to ride as she'd intended, she had to wait until someone demonstrated every little detail before her ability adapted.

Sabrina rubbed her stiff neck and shoulders. It was too late to add a clause to the spell that would have prevented the aches and pains inherent in any new physical activity. "I think every muscle and bone in my body hurts."

"Aspirin and a hot bath will help," Zelda/Glenda advised. "As soon as possible."

"But you should never take aspirin on an empty stomach." Salem hooked a paper napkin with one claw and pulled it out of the metal holder. "Didn't somebody say something about doughnuts?"

"Coming right up." Zelda/Glenda shoved her order pad into her apron pocket. Swallowing hard, she slowly pulled out a fistful of bills, change, and order slips. "Oops."

"Oops?" Hilda's head snapped up from the worksheet lying on the counter by the cash register. "Please, don't tell me you forgot to ring up some of your orders *again!*"

"I forgot." Flinching, Zelda/Glenda held up three wrinkled order slips. "I was busing tables, and it just slipped my mind."

"That's no excuse!" Furious, Hilda waved the tally sheet. "I'm almost done figuring out today's receipts! Now I'll have to cash out and count everything all over again."

"Oh, no, you won't!" Zelda/Glenda's face darkened as she separated the cash from the orders. She shoved the bills and assorted coins into her jeans pocket. "I'll just *keep* this money as compensation for *your* insensitive, contemptuous attitude! All you've done for the past two days is insult me, Hilda."

"No, I've just tried to correct your mistakes," Hilda said, losing control as she spoke. "Before your incompetence drives me out of business!"

"I take it this arrangement isn't going too well," Sabrina said, hoping to infuse the volatile situation with a measure of calm.

"I'm doing the best I can!" Zelda/Glenda fumed.

"Which is costing *me* a small fortune in lost revenue!" Hilda stormed over to the table and snatched the order slips out of Zelda/Glenda's hand. "How many customers walked out without paying today because you forgot to *give* them their checks?"

"Okay, that's it!" Zelda/Glenda ripped off her apron

and shoved it into Hilda's hands. Removing her disguise with a quick point, Zelda stomped toward the door. "Glenda quits!"

"So who's going to work tomorrow?" Hilda asked as Zelda unlocked the door to leave.

"I haven't decided, yet!" Zelda stepped outside and turned to face them with an indignant toss of her head. "Good night!" She slammed the door.

"And good riddance to Glenda," Hilda muttered, sighing.

"Maybe *now* I can get some decent help."

Sabrina blinked, bewildered. "But won't the new help *still* be Aunt Zelda?"

"Glenda, Zelda, somebody . . . pleeaase . . . feed the cat!" Salem dropped his head onto the table with a *thunk* to emphasize his famished condition.

"I'll get the doughnuts," said Sabrina as she headed toward the counter. Every once in a while she longed for a mortal's mundane existence, where life was never complicated by talking horses with career conflicts, an aunt who could change personas as easily as most people changed clothes, or a manipulative cat who needed to attend a few meetings of Bored and Incorrigible Anonymous.

Chapter 6

"**J**osh!" Hilda collapsed in a chair as Josh arrived for his afternoon and evening shift. She swept the dirty dishes on the table aside and propped her chin in her hands. "Boy, am I glad to see you."

"Tough day?" Josh stopped to clear the table on his way to the back room to clock in.

"You could say that." Hilda blew a wisp of hair out of her eyes and stared at an uneaten blueberry muffin a customer had left. "Those cost four dollars a dozen wholesale. Too bad there are laws against reusing perfectly good untouched food."

"I'm sure that muffin won't be around to torment you for long," Josh said. "Cousin Matilda will swoop in to devour it any second now."

"No, she won't." Hilda sighed. Zelda/Matilda had reported to work the day after Zelda/Glenda quit.

"Matilda quit this morning." Rising, Hilda picked up the remaining dishes and followed Josh to the sink.

"She did?" Josh struggled not to grin. "That's a shame."

"Hmph." Hilda poured herself a cup of black coffee.

"So she's consuming someone else's profit margin now, huh?" Josh asked as he put the dishes in the dishwasher.

"Or she vanished into thin air," Hilda quipped.

"So you've been handling things alone all day?" Josh sounded almost hopeful as he scanned the floor, looking for another new waitress. Although he was officially the manager, Glenda and Matilda had both used Josh as the complaint department for family squabbles thinly veiled as management-labor disputes. Being the middleman with sympathies on both sides had put him in an awkward position he wouldn't miss.

If Josh is sick of fake Spellman cousins as relief servers, Hilda thought, *he's out of luck.*

"No, I've had help." Hilda swept her hand toward the back room as though introducing a stage performer. "Meet Cousin Zeke."

"Yo! You must be Josh." Zelda/Zeke burst out of the back room and grabbed Josh's hand. Disguised as a short, middle-aged man with thinning blond hair, a flabby stomach, and a bald spot, Zelda/Zeke vigorously pumped the stricken manager's hand. "Glad to meet you, boy!"

"Likewise, I'm sure," Josh said with a distinct lack of sincerity. "Are you just getting off work?"

Yes, Hilda thought with relief. Since Zelda had a physics class to teach, Cousin Zeke had to leave. *And*

I'll save at least ten dollars in damages between now and closing because Zeke won't be here.

"Yep. Gotta go." Zelda/Zeke nodded and smoothed a blond handlebar mustache. Then, hitching up baggy red pants held on with purple suspenders over a bright yellow shirt, he grabbed three apples from a bowl on the counter.

"This one has an appetite, too, huh?" Josh glanced at Hilda with both eyebrows cocked in disbelief.

"Could I be that lucky?" Hilda asked, wallowing in sarcasm. She quickly improvised an explanation for the new cousin's bizarre behavior as Zelda/Zeke began juggling the apples. "Zeke has never been able to accept flunking out of clown college so he's stuck in perpetual audition mode."

"Well, that might be entertaining," Josh said, folding his arms with a wan smile.

"Optimist," Hilda mumbled as Zelda/Zeke juggled her way toward the door. After the first two hours of working with Zelda/Zeke, Hilda realized that the monetary hit incurred by Zelda's disguise personas got worse with each new manifestation. Hilda had spent more money on Matilda's food than Glenda had failed to collect or ring up. The cost of Zeke's damages would equal Matilda's food bill by close tomorrow. Hilda couldn't afford to criticize the clumsy wannabe clown because he might quit, and then she'd be stuck with a *worse* phony Zelda cousin.

Roxie and Miles came into the coffeehouse and paused, gawking as Zelda/Zeke stopped to juggle the apples faster and faster. The few midafternoon customers began to clap, urging the waiter on. Mesmerized, Roxie, Miles, and Josh were all taken by surprise when the potbellied little man suddenly threw *all* the apples upward and yelled, "Catch!"

Roxie squealed and threw her arms over her head when she ducked. One of the apples landed on the floor by her feet, squashed to a pulp on impact.

"Splatter much!" Miles laughed.

"Not funny!" Hilda pointed, deflecting a second apple so it zoomed toward Miles and lodged in his mouth.

Josh caught the third and tossed it back to Zelda/Zeke.

"Bombs away!" Zelda/Zeke stretched out the waistband of her baggy pants, caught the apple inside, let the waistband snap back, and executed a deep bow to another round of halfhearted applause. "Thank you, thank you. Parting is such sweet sorrow, but I'm out of here until tomorrow!"

Miles took a bite of the apple in his mouth, frowned, and blocked Zelda/Zeke's exit. "You look awfully familiar. Do I know you?"

"Ever been to Pooh-dinky, Mars?" Zelda/Zeke asked in a gravelly voice.

"No, don't think so." Miles shook his head, then brightened. "Unless I was abducted by aliens in my sleep and my memories are still suppressed."

"Never saw you before in my life." Zelda/Zeke pushed out the door and was gone.

"That'll be a dollar fifty," Hilda said when Roxie and Miles reached the counter. She couldn't recover the cost of the smashed apple or the one Zelda/Zeke had taken away in his pants, but the kid was eating the third one.

"For this?" Miles raised the partially eaten apple. "Not a chance. That guy threw it at me. Consider it combat pay."

"All right. I'm too frazzled to argue." Hilda turned to vent her frustration on Roxie. If Roxie had agreed to work in Sabrina's absence, she wouldn't be going broke employing the many faces of Zelda. "So you're too busy to work here, but not too busy to hang out?"

"I'm here to do my homework." Roxie grimaced. "I will be *so* glad when Sabrina is done with that horse riding thing. Our room smells like a barn. Gag."

"You think that's a problem?" Hilda reached under the counter and pulled out a bus tub full of broken cups and saucers. "Zeke just learned how to juggle today."

"If it's okay with you, Mike, I'd like to ride a little longer." Sitting astride George in the lesson ring, Sabrina leaned over to pat the horse's neck. After riding every day for a week, she was relaxed, comfortable, and confident. Even with the "show me" requirement she had mistakenly built into the ability chant, the spell was working perfectly. "You're not tired, are you, boy?"

George shook his head no.

Sabrina grinned. The horse's overall mood had improved in direct proportion to her equitation expertise. Even he was enjoying the lessons now.

In an effort to accommodate everyone's academic schedules, Mike had scheduled the riding class early today. Since Sabrina didn't have any other obligations, she didn't want to waste the rest of the afternoon. The Westbridge Hunt Club Horse Show was next Saturday, only five days away, and she wanted to make sure she had the basics down before she asked Mike about competing.

"That is so weird." Carol looked back at Sabrina as she reined Pepper to a halt by the gate. "Maybe talking to George all the time really does have a positive effect."

"I don't know if it helps, but it doesn't hurt." Sabrina shrugged. Everyone assumed George's uncanny responses to her verbal questions and comments were cute and accidental, which was fine with her.

"I wish I could get that angle thingie right." Toni sighed with frustration. "I think I'll stay a little longer, too. I've got time before my next class."

"Do you mean diagonal?" Mike asked.

"Yeah, that's it." Toni nudged Cameo with her heel to keep her moving past the open gate instead of following Pepper out of the ring.

"You two have fun." Mike closed the gate when Pepper was clear and waved as he backed off toward the barn. "I'll check to see how you're doing after the other horses are settled."

Sabrina waited in the center of the ring as Toni urged Cameo into a trot along the rail. Faster than a walk, the trot was an extremely bouncy, up-and-down gait. If the horse was jogging, a slow or sitting trot, it was easy to stay in the saddle. However, most English horses had a longer stride that required the rider to post, the term for moving off the saddle and back down again to avoid being bounced.

"Want some help, Toni?" Sabrina asked, sharing the other girl's frustration with a pinch of guilt thrown in. She had become an accomplished rider at the walk, trot, and canter because she had the advantage of the ability spell. That didn't make her an expert, but it was hard to watch Toni struggle with the finer aspects of equitation that she had learned so easily.

Like diagonals, Sabrina thought as Toni and Cameo moved around the ring. When riding at a trot in a circle, the rider was supposed to be off the saddle when the horse's outside front leg, the leg farthest away from the center, was forward. The rider sat down when the outside front leg moved back. Being on the correct diagonal was not essential for pleasure riding, but it was imperative in the show ring.

Like Carol, Toni was athletic and a quick learner. Although she didn't have the polished command the ability spell had given Sabrina, Toni and Carol had both expressed interest in entering the horse show, too. Their chances of winning a ribbon were slimmer than George's, but Toni wouldn't be competitive at all unless she mastered diagonals.

"Boy, would I!" Toni looked at Cameo's outside shoulder. She was rising out of the saddle when

Cameo's outside front leg was back. "I know I'm wrong, but I just can't seem to switch!"

"Just sit in the saddle for an extra bounce!" Sabrina shouted and held her breath when Toni stopped posting. Watching Cameo's shoulder, the dark-haired girl waited three strides before she began posting again, but she still ended up on the wrong diagonal. Sabrina didn't have a clue how to help correct Toni's problem.

"Sorry, Cameo." Toni brought the little palomino mare down to a walk. "But I am *not* leaving this ring until I learn how to do this."

"Psst!" George whispered to get Sabrina's attention. "What is so difficult about up, down, up, down, down, up?"

"Run that by me again," Sabrina asked, confused.

"I'll show you." Without waiting for Sabrina to cue him, George moved toward the fence. He began to trot as soon as she shortened up on the reins. "Do *not* watch my shoulder, okay? Just listen and do as I *say* while you post."

"Okay." Fixing her gaze between George's ears, Sabrina rose and fell in sync with the horse's stride and voice.

"Up, down, up, down, *down,* up, down," the horse said. "The trick is not to *look.*"

"Got it!" Sabrina had switched to the wrong diagonal when George had uttered two *downs* in a row. Sitting another double-down to switch back, she trotted George up beside Cameo to explain the horse's method to Toni. Within five minutes, Toni was switching diagonals back and forth with ease.

"I can't believe I was having so much trouble!" Thrilled, Toni laughed as she stopped Cameo and slipped to the ground to open the gate. "Or that I was afraid to ride that first day. Thanks for the help, Sabrina. Now that I'm getting the hang of this, I love it."

"Me, too," Sabrina agreed. Not all the girls had caught on as quickly or enjoyed riding as much as Carol and Toni, but they all liked each other, the horses, and the work. The fresh air and physical exertion was a welcome break from the mental pressures of studying inside the hallowed halls of Adams College.

"Let me know what Mike says about this weekend, okay?" Toni asked as she led Cameo out of the ring.

"I'll talk to him today," Sabrina said. When she had explained Mike's no-pay-for-teaching situation to the rest of the class, they had elected her to handle Operation Horse Show. If Mike agreed to let Sabrina, Toni, and Carol enter, Dixie, Beth, and Gretchen would work as grooms, gophers, cheerleaders, and whatever else Mike needed them to do. Everyone was excited about the possibility of participating.

"Good," Toni said. "I think Carol is more anxious to show than you and I are!"

"Show?" Debra's voice repeated.

Sabrina's heart sank when she looked up to see Debra, Cindy, and Veronica riding toward the ring. As usual, their horses and their tack gleamed, and they were all wearing immaculate riding attire and polished boots.

"Are you talking about the Westbridge Hunt Club

79

Horse Show this weekend?" Debra asked. Golden Wings, the girl's chestnut mare and the object of George's affections, pawed the ground when Debra brought her to a halt by the open gate.

George tucked his chin and arched his neck, a demonstration of equine muscle flexing that seemed to leave Goldie cold. The mare snorted and looked away.

"Yeah, why?" Holding the end of Cameo's reins, Toni self-consciously crossed her arms over her dirt-streaked T-shirt. After the first day, the beginning equitation class had started wearing old shirts, jeans, and sports shoes to do the stable chores. They changed into boots, britches, or chaps over jeans to ride, but they no longer looked like models of high horse fashion.

"You're *not* thinking of entering, are you?" Debra glanced from Toni to Sabrina, obviously appalled by the idea.

Startled by the direct confrontation, Sabrina hesitated. Everything around her seemed to shift into slow motion.

Cindy stopped her dark brown gelding, Moon Shadow, farther up the fence. Crazy Quilt, a dappled gray mare, fidgeted until Veronica moved her closer to Moon Shadow. Both girls were curious, but apparently preferred to watch and listen without becoming directly involved in the discussion.

From the corner of her eye, Sabrina saw Salem come to attention in his ringside seat. On the far end of the ring, a brush jump had been inserted into one section of fence instead of three white rails. Except when something interesting was going on, like now, Salem spent most of the lessons curled up and dozing in the fake greenery that topped the white, two-foot-high obstacle.

"Yes, we are," Sabrina answered finally, meeting Debra's uncompromising gaze. Her palms began to sweat, but she checked an impulse to wipe her hands on her new leather chaps. "I've got a blank spot on my bulletin board that's just screaming for one of those fancy rosette ribbons, preferably blue."

"In your dreams, Sabrina! I mean, you've only been riding a week." Debra shifted in her saddle. She looked flustered, as though she simply couldn't process the idea that a common equitation student would dare invade the elite realm of the Westbridge Hunt Club Horse Show. "And *what* are you going to ride? That *school* horse?"

"Absolutely. Mission Impossible is perfectly capable of doing"—Sabrina was thrown off-balance when George decided to take matters into his own hooves and moved smartly to the rail—"everything your horse can do!"

"Oh, really? I wouldn't be so sure about that." Incensed and insulted, Debra rode Goldie into the ring and positioned herself on the rail opposite Sabrina.

"Are *you* in for a rude awakening, girlie," George muttered.

Oh, boy, Sabrina thought as the horse collected himself underneath her. George would never forgive her if she refused Debra's challenge and shamed him in front of Goldie. She just hoped she didn't forget everything she had learned when the pressure was on. *But better to find out now than next Saturday in the horse show ring!*

"Go, Sabrina!" Toni called, closing the gate.

"This should be interesting," Cindy said to Veronica as Sabrina and George rode by their position.

"Not interesting enough, though." Veronica sat with her feet dangling free of the stirrups, resting her crossed arms on the front of her saddle. "Don't tell Debra I said so, but it wouldn't hurt her to get beaten by *somebody*."

How odd, Sabrina thought as she watched Debra gather her reins. She had suspected that Cindy and Veronica weren't entirely pleased with Debra's arrogant attitude, either. Their latest comments seemed to prove it. Bolstered by the unexpected and indirect support, Sabrina concentrated on riding, matching Debra's moves and graceful style.

"Looking good," Salem said as Sabrina and George trotted past his perch in the brush jump. "Don't screw it up, Sabrina."

"Ignore the cat. We're doing great, aren't we, George?" Sabrina asked anxiously as they rounded the far corner where no one else could hear.

"Yeah, but Debra is probably going to canter, and we're moving to the left." A nervous tremor infected George's voice. "This is my bad lead."

"Oh, right. I forgot." Sabrina braced herself to help the horse. The canter was a rocking, three-beat gait that was easy for the rider to sit. However, when George was cantering to the left in a circle, his left front leg had to support all his weight to keep him properly balanced. The opposite was true if he was cantering to the right. For some reason, George had no problem catching his right lead, but he had trouble getting the left lead on his first stride.

"Let's *go,* Debra!" Cindy yelled, cupping her hands around her mouth. "Edward expects us to be warmed up when he gets to the ring!"

"In a minute!" Debra scowled as she brought Goldie back down to a walk. It wasn't hard to tell that she was upset because Sabrina and George hadn't backed out yet.

Grinning broadly, Toni gave Sabrina a thumbs-up.

When Goldie broke into a canter, Sabrina and George were both ready. Sabrina subtly shifted her weight to the right and cued George with a nudge to his right side. He immediately started to canter, leading off with his left leg.

"Woohoo!" Sabrina couldn't help feeling exuberant as George carried her around the rectangular enclosure. Riding was a blast, but the "complete horse experience" had gone far beyond just passing a course and having a good time. She and George were a team.

With a mission, Sabrina reminded herself.

"We're leaving, Debra!" Veronica slipped her feet into her stirrups and walked Crazy Quilt toward the larger ring farther up the meadow.

Cindy gave Sabrina a casual wave as Moon Shadow fell into step behind Veronica's gray mare.

"Follow *this!*" Debra glared at Sabrina as she cantered Goldie up the center of the ring.

Touched by Cindy's gesture, Sabrina wasn't paying close attention. She turned George to follow Goldie without realizing what Debra intended to do until it was almost too late.

Debra did not turn Goldie when they reached the fence. The horse lifted off the ground on powerful haunches, sailed over the brush jump and a terrified cat, and continued across the meadow toward the upper ring.

Frozen in shock, Salem stared with widening eyes as Sabrina and George charged toward him.

"Piece of cake," George muttered. He barreled toward the jump with his ears perked forward and every muscle primed for takeoff.

"Oh, no!" Regaining her stalled wits, Sabrina pulled back on the reins.

"What's the matter?" George sputtered as he slid to a stop. "We could have made that jump easy!"

"Not!" Sabrina backed George away from the fence, asserting her own stubborn streak.

"Did all my fur just turn white with fright?" Salem asked, eyeing the deep gouges his claws had made in the wooden bars of the jump.

"Not? What's that mean?" Agitated, George started to prance and champ at the bit.

"It means I signed up to learn to ride," Sabrina said smiling. Mike hadn't shown her how to jump yet, and even with the ability spell in effect, she wasn't sure she wanted to know. "Nobody said anything about cruising at low altitude."

Chapter 7

George was depressed the next day when Sabrina arrived at the stables early.

"I'm sorry, George," Sabrina said as she ran a soft bristle brush over the horse's chocolate brown coat. She hadn't meant to embarrass George in front of Goldie yesterday afternoon. She just hadn't been prepared to leap a two-foot planter in a single bound on two thousand pounds of airborne horse.

"Sabrina really is sorry," Salem said from the feed bin. "Sorry and scared stiff."

"That doesn't help me, does it?" George addressed the cat, ignoring Sabrina. "Goldie will never speak to me again."

"Goldie has *never* spoken to you," Salem pointed out.

"And now she never will!" George stomped a back hoof and flicked his tail.

Sabrina tossed the brush in the grooming box. She didn't blame George for being upset. She wasn't happy about letting Debra get the best of *her,* either, but it would have been foolish to risk jumping before she had had a jumping lesson.

"Hi, Sabrina! You're early." Mike walked into the barn with a bridle slung over his shoulder. He paused to smile at her through the bars in the stall door. "But I'm not complaining."

Sabrina smiled back, pleased that Mike seemed really glad to see her. She was sure she'd really like Mike if she got to know him better. He just hadn't made a move yet, and she had sworn off using magic to enhance her social life, for now anyway. When it came to romance, there was no magical substitute for the real thing.

"I wanted to talk to you about the horse show." Sabrina picked up the grooming box and slipped out of the stall. Freezing on the jump had upset her, too, and she hadn't felt like talking to Mike about the upcoming show the previous afternoon. But the event was only four days away. If Mike agreed to let her, Toni, and Carol enter, they had to start getting ready now.

"The Westbridge Hunt Club Horse Show on Saturday?" Mike hung the bridle in the tack room, then sat on a hay bale in the aisle outside the tack room door. "You're not really serious about entering, are you?"

"Yeah, I am." Sabrina sat down beside Mike. Resting her forearms on her thighs, she nervously clasped her hands. Sitting so close to Mike made it difficult to concentrate on the conversation, but everyone was counting on her to make the point and win any ensuing arguments. "Toni and Carol want to enter, too, and the other girls have all volunteered to groom, clean tack, and walk the horses between classes. Whatever we need."

"Why?" Mike seemed genuinely perplexed.

"Because we *all* think you should be getting *paid* to teach," Sabrina said. "We can't promise to win or even that we won't mess up, but we're willing to try so the college administrator will see that you deserve a raise."

"Wow." Mike inhaled deeply and ran a hand through his dark, wavy hair. "I don't know what to say."

Sabrina tilted her head, issuing a challenge. "Well, I guess it depends on whether or not you're willing to put your reputation on the line for a bunch of beginners."

Mike hesitated, which Sabrina took as a good sign because he didn't dismiss the idea without considering it.

"And George," Sabrina added.

"George?" Mike frowned.

"Right." Sabrina couldn't tell Mike about her deal with the horse, but she was honor bound to represent George's interests in the horse show, too. He had more at stake than anyone. "Edward won't know that George should be a show horse unless George proves it."

"Wait a second." Mike held up a hand. "You and Toni and Carol can probably go in novice equitation on the flat without humiliating yourselves or me, but—"

"The flat?" Sabrina interrupted to question the term.

"Walk, trot, and canter both ways of the ring," Mike explained, "as opposed to equitation over fences, which is jumping."

"Cool!" Sabrina beamed, relieved. She still wasn't

comfortable with the concept of playing leapfrog with heavy horses and solid fences. "We can all handle that flat stuff, no problem."

"Yeah, but to prove that George is a show horse you'd have to show him in the Green Hunter Division." Mike nodded, rubbing his chin and thinking aloud. "George moves well enough, but I've never bothered to find out what he can really do."

Now Sabrina frowned. "What's a green hunter?"

"A novice is a beginning rider, and the rider's ability is judged in an equitation class," Mike said. "A beginning horse is called green, and the horse is judged in hunter classes. A good hunter should have an even disposition and a steady way of going."

Sabrina knew George had the steady moves, but his only claim to having an *even* disposition was that he was *usually* cranky.

"But since you seem to bring out the best in George, you might be able to pull it off." Mike looked at Sabrina with a mischievous grin. "The show's in four days, so I guess it *really* depends on whether or not you're up for a crash course in riding a hunter over fences."

"You mean *jumping* fences?" Sabrina swallowed hard, stunned.

With a sudden flash of insight, Sabrina realized that ability wasn't the reason she didn't want to jump. Once Mike demonstrated the technique, the spell would kick in and she would know how to ride over fences. She was worried because she didn't have any control over *George's* ability! The horse seemed confident, but guys who wanted to show off for girls often overestimated themselves. If George messed up hurling himself over a jump to impress Golden Wings, they might both fall.

And they could both be hurt.

"Little fences." Mike held his hand about two feet off the ground. However, when he realized Sabrina seemed to have reservations, he decided not to push. "Look, you don't have to decide right this minute, Sabrina. I've got another idea."

"Lunch?" Sabrina asked in jest, but with a measure of hope.

"I'd love to go to lunch with you sometime, Sabrina, but that's not what I had in mind." Rising, Mike looked at his watch. "The others won't be here for another hour so why don't you and I go for a short trail ride? It would be a nice change of pace for everyone. Even George."

"I love that idea!" Sabrina accepted with an enthusiasm the horse didn't share. George complained the whole time she was tacking up.

"For your information, forest trails are not a picnic." George hung his head in protest as Sabrina led him out of the barn. Mike was still getting Pepper ready for the outing. "Trails are littered with rocks and sticks that can hurt your feet and they're lined with branches that snap in your face."

"Well, you'll just have to deal," Sabrina said, losing patience. Going on a trail ride with Mike was an unexpected bonus. She wasn't going to let George's sour attitude spoil it. "I'm sure a few rocks and branches didn't bother your wild ancestors."

"Probably not," George agreed sarcastically. "My earliest ancestors were born and raised on the Sahara Desert where there *weren't* any rocks and branches."

Sabrina checked the girth that held the saddle in place. The leather strap seemed tight, but Salem thought George might want to get even for her embarrassing refusal to jump yesterday. "Are you holding air to bloat yourself?"

"Now why would I do that?" George asked.

"So when you exhale the girth will be loose," Sabrina said, repeating what Salem had told her. "Then I'll look like a fool when I try to get on and the saddle slips."

George slowly turned his head to look at her. "I would never do *anything* that would hurt you, Sabrina. Where did you get such an idea?"

The horse sounded so hurt, Sabrina felt like a jerk. "From a cat who knows every trick in the book and figures *everyone* must be just as devious and spiteful as he is sometimes."

"Ready?" Mike walked up leading Pepper, ending Sabrina's conversation with George.

"Can't wait." Smiling, Sabrina led George to the tree stump by the lesson barn that served as a mounting block. She whispered in his ear just before she got on. "Please accept my apologies, George. For everything."

"Okay," George said softly, "but you've got to trust me. I won't let anything bad happen to you."

"All right." Sabrina gave the horse a quick pat on the neck then swung her leg over the saddle. She shot Mike another smile as he moved Pepper toward the meadow at a brisk walk. "Here we go, George. Force yourself to have a good time."

"If you insist." George sighed as he followed Mike into the woods.

Sabrina had enjoyed learning to ride in the ring, but touring the forest on horseback put the "whole horse experience" in a completely different perspective. Instead of being intent on form and function as she rode George in monotonous, endless circles, she relaxed and tuned into the horse and everything around her. Her senses, dulled by constant exposure to a manufactured world of steel and cement, were awakened in the wilderness setting.

Her nostrils flared, teased by the musty scent of damp leaves combined with the sharp tang of pine and oiled leather. Dust motes shimmered in shafts of sunlight that filtered through the trees and highlighted toadstools, ferns, and wildflowers. Layers of pine needles and leaves that cushioned the trail muted the sound of George's hooves, and water gurgled around partially submerged logs and rocks in a nearby creek. Sabrina's heart swelled with a sense of profound peace that rose from within and was amplified by the beauty and wonder of her surroundings.

"How are you doing back there?" Mike called out as Pepper sidestepped to skirt a large puddle. George just splashed through it.

"Great!" Sabrina had adopted a more casual, cowboy style, resting her right hand on her thigh and holding the reins loosely in her left. She had to duck to avoid a small branch here and there, but the bridle path was obviously maintained and kept free of obstacles. "It's beautiful out here."

"I think so, too." Mike rose out of his saddle and swiveled to look back. "How about we step up the pace?"

"Sure!" Sabrina didn't hesitate, trusting George to mind his manners and his footing. As the horse eased into a trot, she was amazed at how smoothly he moved on the springy trail. Posting required almost no effort at all, and she settled into the easy rhythm as though she'd been riding all her life.

When the trees began to thin out, Mike reined Pepper to a stop and pointed toward a large clearing several yards ahead. "If you want to canter, this is the place to do it. The trail stays pretty straight through that meadow and the woods on the other side."

"I'm game." Sabrina grinned. "Tally ho and all that."

"I kind of figured you'd say that. Well, not the 'tally ho' part." Mike grinned.

"Sorry. I got carried away." Sabrina shrugged.

"Well, if you really want to get carried away and let George stretch his legs, move off his back a little so he's running under you." Mike lifted off the saddle, leaning forward slightly to demonstrate.

Sabrina mimicked the move and asked, "What's the point to this?"

"It's called a hand-gallop position," Mike said, sitting back down. "It saves some wear and tear on the posterior, and sometimes they ask for it in the hunter hack class. That's just like equitation on the flat," he explained, anticipating Sabrina's question, "except they're judging the horse, not the rider."

"Got it." Sabrina nodded with a conviction she didn't feel. She didn't want to admit to herself or Mike and George that she was afraid to jump, but she was. Somehow, she *had* to get over it or she couldn't show George as a hunter. That, however, was easier said than done. No witch had ever devised a spell that could eliminate genuine fear. "Can I ask you something?"

"Sure."

"Do most horses know what they're doing?" Sabrina noted Mike's surprise and realized he might have been expecting another invitation to lunch. She quickly clarified, making a mental note to follow up on the lunch issue after the horse show. "I mean, take a jump, for instance. Does the horse go for it even if the fence is too high and he might not make it?"

George snorted and shook his head, obviously insulted by the inquiry. Sabrina ignored her mount's objection. She wasn't sure she could trust his judgment when Goldie was involved, and Debra would be showing Golden Wings on Saturday.

Mike paused to give the question serious thought. "To be honest, most people would never ask a horse to do anything beyond its capabilities. Even so, sometimes a horse doesn't get off right so it doesn't clear the jump."

"And they fall?" Sabrina winced.

"Not very often," Mike assured her. "The *jumps* are designed to fall apart if the horse hits them with a hoof going over. Of course, sometimes a horse refuses to jump. Then the rider falls off when the horse stops."

"That's what I was afraid of." Sabrina sighed. Catching another curious glance from Mike, she picked up her reins and forced a smile. "Ready whenever you are."

"Follow me." Mike urged Pepper into a slow canter.

"I'm not incompetent," George hissed, hanging back as Pepper moved away. "I told you I wouldn't let anything bad happen. I thought you were going to trust me?"

"Can we discuss this back at the barn, please?" Sabrina saw Mike and Pepper break out of the woods into the meadow, and she didn't want to be left too far behind.

"I suppose so," George said grudgingly. "Hang on."

Sabrina lurched when George took off, but she quickly regained her seat. Shifting forward as the horse lengthened his stride she had no trouble maintaining her balance at the faster gallop. With the wind and ground whipping past as George charged across the clearing, every moment was a joyous triumph for Sabrina. Except that a nagging thought kept popping up: Mike and George both knew she was afraid to jump, and George was taking it personally.

Sabrina rode on autopilot as George closed the distance between him and Pepper. When Mike and Pepper veered to the left and George followed, she didn't question the sudden deviation in course even though Mike had said the trail went straight. She was just a passenger as the horse thundered toward the trees.

Trailing Mike's big, dark brown gelding by several feet, Sabrina didn't see the giant log lying across the path until Pepper popped over it.

By then it was too late to stop.

As George left the ground, Sabrina instinctively moved farther forward, adjusting her weight over the horse's shifting center of gravity. Her spirits soared as the horse flew, and when George's feet hit the ground on the far side, her heart and pulse were pounding with an adrenaline rush. She hadn't experienced anything that thrilling since her first flying tour of Westbridge on a magic vacuum cleaner.

"We jumped!" Sabrina's heart was still racing when she brought George to a halt beside Mike. She stared at the fallen tree, which was at least two feet high and absolutely solid. "We jumped that log!"

"Imagine that." George looked at her solemnly, trying desperately not to laugh.

"You did that on purpose!" Sabrina suddenly realized that Mike had planned the log jump ambush when he suggested the trail ride.

"Yes," Mike confessed, "but I'm *not* sorry. With your natural talent, Sabrina, jumping a log or a two-foot green hunter fence isn't a big deal."

"It was a big deal to me." Sabrina protested.

"It was all in your head," Mike insisted. "The *idea* of jumping scares most new riders—until they survive the Michael Santori Log-on-the-Trail Maneuver."

"Then I bet most of them want to jump it again, huh?" Sabrina grinned. She wasn't even a little bit mad at Mike. His insight into human nature and his simple solution for curing a silly fear made him a great teacher.

"Usually." Mike smiled, obviously delighted that his ploy had worked.

George raised his head and curled his lip back in a horselaugh. Sabrina couldn't tell if he was enjoying the joke on her, relieved that she had overcome her fear of jumping, or both. Either way, he might be in a better mood for the next few days.

"If you're still game," Mike said, his dark eyes twinkling, "I know the location of every jumpable fallen tree and low fence in the woods."

Sabrina had no intention of backing down from the implied dare or turning down a chance to jump again. The exhilaration of flying through the woods and sailing over logs on a horse she trusted implicitly just couldn't be duplicated. It was what George had been born to do, and she couldn't wait to share a moment of mutual glory.

"Let's do it." Sabrina winked as she gathered her reins. "Tally ho and woohoo!"

Chapter 8

Friday afternoon Sabrina stood by the gate to the lesson arena, waiting for Mike to finish setting up the jumps. The other girls were standing by the fence talking, walking their horses, or letting the animals graze. Although only Toni and Carol had decided to enter the novice equitation class at the Westbridge Hunt Club Horse Show tomorrow, they had all participated in Mike's practice flat class. And they were all infected with an excited sense of urgency he called "horse show fever."

"How can you be so calm?" Sabrina whispered in George's ear as she scratched his chin.

"It's not hard when you've got three square meals a day, a warm bed, and no responsibilities," Salem muttered. He sat on a fence post, silently supervising Mike's activities.

"I was talking to George." Sabrina glanced past the cat into the ring as Mike raised the rail on the gate jump. This would be her last practice trip over fences before the show. She wouldn't suffer any lasting ill effects if she messed up, but George's whole existence depended on how well they performed the next day.

"Would it help if I acted like a nervous dingbat?" George flicked an ear to chase a fly and shifted his weight to his right hind leg.

"Probably not." Sabrina sighed.

"Good. Wake me when Mike is ready." George yawned, his head drooping as he drifted back into a standing doze.

Salem noted George's tranquil state with skepticism. "Calm is one thing, but he's practically comatose."

"Which is better than being a basket case." With the reins loosely clutched in one hand, Sabrina leaned on the rails to study the course. After three days of intense training under the influence of the ability spell, jumping had become a snap. However, there was a lot more to showing than just getting over the fences.

Like George and I could be disqualified for being off course, Sabrina thought with a knot in her stomach. Everyone had to take the fences in the same order in the jumping classes, and the order was different for every class. She only had to worry about the Green Hunter Over Fences course, but the diagram wouldn't be available until tomorrow morning at the show.

"How are your nerves, Sabrina?" Toni walked over, leading Cameo. "I can't wait to show, but I just know I'll get a major case of the shakes tomorrow."

"I can *so* sympathize." Sabrina held up her hand for a

high five. No matter what happened in the show ring, she was already a winner because of the new friends she had made. That didn't count with the college administration and Edward, however. Only winning ribbons would convince them that George and Mike were worth more than they gave them credit for.

Sabrina and Toni were so intent on watching Mike, they didn't notice Cindy ride up until she spoke.

"So you're really going to ride in the Westbridge Hunt Club Horse Show tomorrow?" Cindy stopped Moon Shadow beside Cameo and gave Toni a quizzical look.

Sabrina turned, shielding her eyes with her hand against the glare of the afternoon sun. She hadn't seen Cindy since Debra had challenged her and George a few days before, and she didn't know what to think about the rich girl's unexpected overture.

"Yeah, we sure are." Cocking her head, Toni crossed her arms in a subtle display of defiance. Since Debra, Cindy, and Veronica had avoided any social contact with the beginning equitation class, Sabrina didn't blame her friend for suspecting Cindy's motives.

"Well, being nervous is the *worst* thing you can do in the show ring," Cindy said, smiling.

Was Cindy really trying to bolster their confidence? Sabrina wondered. *When in doubt, assume the best,* she decided. Although Cindy was Debra's best friend, she had never done or said anything mean. In fact, Sabrina realized, this was not the first time Cindy had made a friendly gesture.

Misinterpreting Sabrina's hesitation, Cindy began to babble in an obvious effort to keep the conversation going. "It's not like Westbridge is a rated show or anything. I mean, nobody's trying to get national points, and the classes aren't clumped in divisions. They just have two types of hunters at these local shows, green and open, instead of a zillion different categories of 'green.'"

"Open?" Toni asked.

"Anybody can enter an open class," Cindy explained. "And you can go in the hunter hack class without *having* to enter the over fences class or visa versa, if you want. The Westbridge show is mostly just for fun."

"*Just* fun?" Sabrina frowned. "I thought that Edward and the college administration *really* want Adams people like you and Debra to win."

"Oh, they do." Cindy shifted in her saddle and shrugged apologetically. "The Westbridge Hunt Club Horse Show is a really big deal around here."

That information didn't do anything to reduce Sabrina's anxiety. "I don't suppose you've got some anti-nervous advice for us first timers, do you?"

"Actually, yes. I do." Leaning forward, Cindy motioned Sabrina and Toni closer. "I was a total wreck before my first over fences class when I was twelve. By the time I went into the ring, even my pony had the jitters. Guess what happened?"

"What?" Sabrina and Toni both asked.

"As I was making my circle, my hard hat slipped down over my eyes. I had to hold my head like this."

Cindy sat up and tilted her head back. "I was so worried about trying to see, I stopped worrying about the jumps."

"That really happened?" Toni asked, aghast.

"Yeah, and my pony came in *third* out of fifteen!" Cindy grinned. "So you might as well relax and have fun at a horse show because you never know when you'll be riding blind."

"That's some of the best advice I've ever gotten," Sabrina said, meaning every word. "Thanks, Cindy."

"Cindy!" Debra hollered as she rode Goldie into the field. She shot her redheaded friend a scathing glance. "Edward's waiting!"

"Gotta go." Rolling her eyes, Cindy reined Moon Shadow toward the upper ring and glanced over her shoulder as they walked away. "Good luck tomorrow."

"Same to you!" Toni shouted as Cindy trotted off. "That was cool, huh?"

"Totally." Sabrina felt her apprehension melt away as Mike waved her into the ring. Nudging George awake, she accepted a leg up from Toni and walked through the gate with her confidence restored.

As Sabrina eased George into a canter and circled to head for the first jump, she relaxed. It was silly for her to be nervous. Between Mike's expertise, hours and hours of practice, and the ability spell—especially the ability spell—she was more than ready to handle a horse show.

She had absolutely nothing to worry about.

* * *

"Are you sure you're not sick, Hilda?" Josh finished wiping down the counter and tossed the rag in the sink.

Hilda decided to put up a brave front. It was Friday night. If business was twice as good as usual, and Roxie didn't eat or break anything, she just might break even for the week. There was no point ruining everyone's weekend by dropping hints that she might not be able to meet the payroll.

"Yeah." Roxie pulled two stacks of paper cups out of a carton and set them by the coffeemaker. "You look a little pale."

"Ill prepared, perhaps, but not sick," Hilda said. "We'll have to use paper cups for in-house and takeout tonight. My supplier couldn't replace all the cups and saucers Cousin Zeke broke until next Monday."

After massive breakage and multiple confrontations, Hilda along with Zeke's growing multitude of fans, finally convinced Zelda that Cousin Zeke's talents were better suited to open mike night than waiting on tables. Since Sabrina would be back on the job Monday and Roxie had agreed to work the weekend shifts, Zelda/Zeke would be making his last coffeehouse appearance in about thirty minutes. There promised to be a big crowd which, hopefully, would help Hilda out of her financial dilemma.

And, Hilda thought with a profound sense of relief, *I won't have to ungainfully employ any more Zelda/fill-in-the-blank cousins.*

"I don't care what the cups look like," Roxie said. "I only agreed to work because I'll make enough in tips to

102

dry clean everything I own. It all reeks of damp straw."

"Well, if you have a wardrobe anywhere near the size of Sabrina's I'll have help for weeks," Hilda offered cheerfully, although her brow was knit with worry.

"Cheer up!" Josh threw one arm around Hilda and the other around Roxie. "It's Friday. All the customers will be so glad it's the end of a long week, they won't mind drinking out of paper cups. And if we're lucky, they won't change their minds when they realize that this clumsiness is also his act and hoot Cousin Zeke off the stage."

They all looked up and saw Miles coming in the door.

"Uh-oh. Here comes trouble," Hilda said.

Roxie waited on Miles. "So do you want something, or are you just afraid to be alone in the house?" she taunted.

"I know I know that Zeke guy, but I don't know why or from where and it's driving me crazy," Miles answered.

"So that would be a no on the coffee?" Roxie asked. She knew Miles wouldn't leave much of a tip anyway and was anxious to move on to someone with real cash.

"I think I'll just sit for a while and see what strikes me," Miles said.

"Probably one of Cousin Zeke's props," Hilda predicted. "Can this night get any worse?"

"Sure." Roxie nodded. "Sabrina could show up in britches and boots, stink up the place, and drive away the paying customers."

"I'm sure Sabrina would go home and change first," Hilda said.

A commotion outside made Josh and Roxie turn in tandem to stare at the front door. Sabrina dragged herself through it, carrying saddlebags and still wearing her riding clothes.

"I'm going to clean the tables on the other side of the room even though they don't need it." Grabbing the damp rag from the sink, Roxie held her nose as she passed Sabrina.

"What are you doing?" Hilda glared at Sabrina and gasped when Salem peeked out from under the saddlebag flap. He grinned sheepishly and waved a paw.

"Stopping for a bite to eat before I go home and collapse," Sabrina said. She seemed completely oblivious to the fact that she reeked of barn and had wisps of hay in her hair. "I just spent three hours cleaning tack and giving George a bath, which he hated, but not as much as he hated having his mane and tail braided. I had no idea a horse show would be so much work."

Hilda leaned over the counter and spoke very softly. "Salem can't be in here."

"He's not in *here*," Sabrina whispered back. "He's *in* my saddlebag."

Hilda knew Sabrina's logic was flawed, but she was just too burdened with other things to press the issue. "You get takeout and you get it as soon as possible so you can both leave."

"Okay. I'm so hungry I'm not even fussy. Just throw something in a bag, and we're out of here." Sabrina smiled with infuriating sweetness, which really annoyed Hilda because it made it impossible to stay mad at her.

"What horse show?" Hilda set a to-go box on the counter and began filling it with scones and muffins.

Sabrina blinked. "Gosh, we've all been so busy I can't believe I didn't tell you!"

"Your coach apparently didn't think it was worth mentioning, either." Hilda scowled at the concealed cat.

"She's riding George in two green hunter classes in the Westbridge Hunt Club Horse Show tomorrow," Salem said through clenched teeth. "And I'm in the mood for something chocolate covered."

"Who's George?" Hilda asked, adding a chocolate-iced doughnut to the box.

"My horse," Sabrina said. "At least, he's mine for the duration of the equitation course. His real name is Mission Impossible, but he prefers George. I have no idea why. He won't say."

"George talks?" Hilda dropped a croissant and fixed Sabrina with a parental authority stare.

"He does now," Salem offered. "And I'll eat that croissant now, if you'll get it off the floor."

"Well, yeah." Sabrina shrugged with a so-what look. "How else was I supposed to find out why he didn't want to work."

"Of course! It's not like you can call in a horse psychic to figure it out," Hilda quipped. "Mortals usually have to guess based on acquired knowledge and use trial and error to find out what's bothering a horse."

"True," Sabrina agreed, "but that's not nearly as efficient as a spell."

"Which completely misses the point." Exasperated, Hilda pressed the other point she found troubling. "You've only been riding for two weeks. How can you possibly be good enough to enter a horse show?"

Sabrina gulped. "Salem *swore* it was okay!"

"It *is*," the cat snapped. "What?"

"Using an ability spell because you want to help someone else?" Sabrina looked away from Hilda's penetrating gaze, no doubt expecting to find out that ability spells were illegal.

They weren't, under certain circumstances.

"Well, Salem was right about that," Hilda said. Sabrina started speaking again before she could finish.

"Boy, is that a relief." Sabrina sagged. "I *had* to learn to ride in a hurry to enter the show. I'm only doing it so Mike can get paid for teaching and George won't get sold to the rental horse stable."

Hilda sighed, wishing there was some way she could soften the blow. Sabrina's intentions were good even if her methods were misguided. "Well, I hope you were paying close attention to what you were doing while you were riding using the ability spell."

Sabrina turned chalk white. "Why?"

"Because you can't use an ability spell in any competition," Hilda said, "or a spell that enhances the horse. Like one that makes him talk."

"Did I forget to mention that?" Salem hunkered down in the saddlebag.

Sabrina stared in shock and continued staring when Zelda raced in. Despite the late hour, Zelda was still dressed in the tailored gray suit she wore to teach.

"Did Cousin Zeke suddenly get stage fright and decide to back out?" Hilda asked nervously. "Because I've already spent money on extra food. And, all those people, Zeke's fans, are expecting him . . . any minute," she added.

Zelda glanced nervously over her shoulder and out the front window. "No, my department faculty meeting ran late, and one of the professors asked me out for coffee. He wouldn't take no for an answer and followed me so I couldn't cast my disguise spell before I got here."

"So where is he?" Hilda closed the box of baked goods and handed it to Sabrina.

"Parking his car. Hello, Sabrina." Zelda cast a quick smile at her stunned niece, then glanced back at Hilda.

"Is he cute?" Hilda quizzed, reverting to habit and temporarily forgetting her financial troubles.

"Very tall, very thin, very bald, very boring," Zelda said quickly, dismissing the pursuing professor as irrelevant. Her next question, however, was posed in frantic earnest. "Should I change in the ladies' room or the men's room?"

Hilda paused, stumped. Since Zelda was a woman and Cousin Zeke was a man, there was no ideal solution. "Well, I guess that depends on whether you want to be embarrassed going in or coming out."

"You're a big help." Spotting Miles just as a tall, thin

man in a rumpled suit walked in, Zelda covered her face with her hand and ducked toward the rest rooms.

Hilda sighed as Sabrina shouldered the cat-filled saddlebags, took the to-go box, and walked toward the door in a zombielike stupor. There was no ideal solution for her problem, either.

Chapter 9

Sabrina had fully intended to break the bad news to George as soon as she got to the barn Saturday morning. However, he was enjoying the extra grain ration in his power breakfast so much she decided to wait. They were in big trouble, but there was no reason to ruin what might be George's last meal as a show horse.

Sabrina, however, couldn't escape thinking about the impending disaster as she helped Carol and Gretchen load saddles and bridles onto the horse van. The speech spell had made George smarter than an ordinary horse, and she couldn't predict how losing his gift for gab would affect his performance. One thing was certain, though. When she reversed the riding ability spell, she would no longer have the skills to help George if *he* spaced everything he had learned in the past two weeks. They would both be outclassed and outsmarted in the show ring.

"How come we couldn't take our horses and all this stuff to the show grounds yesterday, Mike?" Dixie set two grooming boxes down by the water buckets Mike hadn't stowed yet.

Sabrina finished hanging three cleaned and oiled bridles on hooks in the large storage compartment, which was located between the cab and the main body of the truck. Although Mike appeared calm and nonchalant about the show, she could tell he was just as excited as they were. His reputation as a trainer *was* on the line. He just didn't want to put any more pressure on her or the other girls.

"Edward made reservations and paid the stabling charges for the other girls' horses months ago," the instructor explained. "I'm not happy about having to use the van as a base of operations, but there is a positive side to not having stalls at the show."

"What?" Beth dropped her end of a hay bale and sat down on it when Toni dropped the other end. She unwrapped a piece of cinnamon gum and popped it in her mouth, then pushed the paper into her jean pocket. She would throw it away later, a habit that met with everyone's approval.

"No stalls to clean." Mike grinned.

Toni looked at him askance. "Except Debra, Cindy, and Veronica won't be cleaning their horses' stalls. Johnny and the other grooms will."

"Details, details." Mike laughed and picked up the buckets. "Come on, gang. Let's get this show on the road."

While Mike and the other girls finished loading the equipment and supplies, Sabrina went back to George's stall. There was no sense putting off the inevitable. She didn't even want to contemplate *how* dire the dire repercussions might be if she tried to compete without removing the spells. The Witches' Council had a no-mercy policy about the unlawful use of magic for gain.

Salem intercepted her in the aisle. "I wouldn't undo the speech spell on George just yet."

"Why not?" Sabrina asked. "What can he possibly have to say between now and our horse show classes that hasn't already been said?"

"Well, for starters, he could tell you that he's nervous about riding in the van." Salem sat with his tail wrapped over his front paws. The tip twitched, which told Sabrina the cat was really worried and not just trying to be difficult. "Probably not a major problem, as long he can discuss it with you."

"Okay." Sabrina didn't see the harm in postponing again. Competing in the show wouldn't be a problem if George was too afraid of riding in the van to get there. She could calm the horse by reminding him that she had been afraid to jump. That was a perfect example of a foolish, unfounded fear George would understand. "Is that all?"

"As far as I know, but then George is a complex horse," Salem said. "You just never know what might be on his mind."

"What are you really trying to tell me, Salem?"

"As your coach, cat, and faithful familiar, I think you

should keep the horse talking as long as possible."
Salem glanced back toward George's stall. "I just can't
shake the feeling that something else could pop up that
we'll absolutely need to know."

Although Sabrina didn't find Salem's reasoning
particularly comforting, she was secretly glad to have
an excuse to keep George talking as long as possible.
She had enjoyed the horse's company, and she would
miss his sarcastic wit and tough-guy tutoring style.
He was also remarkably rational, she realized, when
she broached the subject of transportation. George
promised to behave after they discussed the relative
safety of highway travel, and to Sabrina's immense relief, he loaded and rode all the way to the show
grounds without mishap.

Everything else went fine when they first arrived,
too. When Mike went to enter Sabrina, Carol, and Toni
in their classes, Salem followed to check out the course
diagrams posted at the show secretary's table. Tied to
the opposite side of the van from Cameo and Pepper,
George quietly nibbled hay while Sabrina groomed and
saddled him. Toni and Gretchen were working as a
team, as were Carol and Beth. When Dixie, who was
helping Sabrina, left to refill George's water bucket,
Sabrina decided she couldn't keep the truth from the
horse any longer. However, just as she was about to explain that they had to lose the spells, Debra Sheridan
rode by on Golden Wings.

They both looked great, Sabrina noted grudgingly.

The mare's chestnut coat gleamed in the morning

sun and the white star on her face almost sparkled. Like George, Cameo, and Pepper, Goldie's flaxen mane was done up in neat braids. The ends of the braids were turned under and tied close to the crest of the horse's neck with colored yarn. Even Goldie's hooves had been coated with a special horse hoof-polishing compound.

Debra wore a navy blue hunt coat over gray britches and a two-inch wide, light pink cloth choker that matched her pink shirt. Not a speck of dust was visible on the black velvet surface of Debra's hard hat or the mirror shine on her black boots.

Sabrina was still dressed in jeans and sneakers. She had planned to change as soon as she finished bridling George.

"I'll give you credit for one thing, Sabrina," Debra said, reining Goldie to a stop. "You sure have a unique sense of humor."

"How do you figure?" Sabrina hated rising to the bait, but she didn't want to be rude, either. There was always a remote chance that Debra was honestly trying to be friendly.

About as likely as a flood on the moon, Sabrina thought. Stranger things had been known to happen, especially in the magical world of witches.

"Goldie, Shadow, and Crazy Quilt are green hunters, Sabrina." Debra chuckled, mocking Sabrina's naïveté. "Most people wouldn't enter a broken-down school horse in a hunter class just to be the butt of a good joke."

Sabrina's cheeks burned with indignation, but she resisted the impulse to strike back verbally. Her only option was to defend George's honor in the show ring.

"Debra!" A tall, handsome man with gray hair waved from a stand of shade trees by the show ring. Wearing gray slacks, an open-neck shirt, and a green cardigan sweater, he was the picture of financial success and personal confidence. "Over here, sweetheart!"

"Hi, Dad!" Dismissing Sabrina without another word, Debra turned Goldie toward her father.

Goldie arched her neck, flicked her tail, and snorted as she pranced by George.

Instead of puffing out his chest, pawing the ground, and snorting back, George heaved a huge sigh and hung his head.

Sabrina quickly checked the immediate area to make sure no one was close enough to overhear, then asked, "What's the matter, George? I may not know a lot about horses, but I'm absolutely certain Goldie was flirting with you!"

"I know!" The horse's head drooped lower. "But she's in the green hunter classes, too. I can't win against Goldie! She might get mad."

"What kind of defeatist attitude is that?" Sabrina asked, appalled. She clasped both sides of his halter and looked him in the eyes. "Believe me, George. Girls love guys who excel, as long as they don't gloat when they win. I'm sure lady horses feel the same way."

"Yeah, but—"

"No buts!" Sabrina pleaded with the horse. "We've got enough strikes against us without you making things worse by throwing the class so you won't upset Golden Wings."

"What strikes?" George's ears twitched with dismay.

Sabrina let go of the halter and sagged against the side of the van. "Last night I found out that I can't use *any* spells in competitions. Not my ability spell or your talking spell."

"I'm doomed!" George gasped.

Last night Sabrina had spent several hours thinking the same thing. However, she had never let a little setback turn her into a quitter before, and it wasn't going to happen now, either.

"Nobody's doomed," Sabrina said. "I may not be able to ride perfectly without the ability spell because I'm a beginner, but you've been a horse your whole life!"

"So?" George scowled.

"They judge the *horse* in hunter classes!" Sabrina threw up her arms. "You've spent the past two weeks telling me you're just as good as Goldie and the other show horses, George. So as long as I don't fall off, I don't see the problem."

"Fall off?" George blinked. "What are the chances of *that* happening?"

"Almost none, maybe." Sabrina shrugged. "Look, I only know one thing for sure, George. We *won't* know if we're a joke or a winning team unless we try. So what's it going to be? Are you going to let Edward sell you to Green Hills as a rental horse without a fight or do we give the green hunter classes the old college try?"

George didn't hesitate. "I can do it if you can, Sabrina."

"Excellent." Sabrina rubbed George under the chin. She wasn't nearly as confident as she wanted George to believe. Her ability to ride was completely dependent on the spell. She was desperately hoping she would retain enough expertise to fake it through the show. "I'll need all the help you can give me, though. Will you remember that when you're not an equine Einstein anymore?"

"I'll remember." George whickered and nuzzled Sabrina's cheek.

"I love you, George." Sabrina hugged the horse's head, then stepped back and raised her finger.

> *Reverse the spells that made me able*
> *And George the talker in the stable.*

Sabrina winced and pointed.

"I hope all those heart-to-heart talks you've had with George help, Sabrina." Water sloshed out of the bucket as Dixie set it down in front of the horse.

"Me, too." Sabrina patted George's neck as he lowered his muzzle to get a drink. Win or lose, all they could do was their best and hope it was good enough.

Salem leaped into Sabrina's arms when she returned from the rest room dressed to ride. "What took you so long?"

"I've been gone ten minutes, tops. Getting dressed for a horse show is almost as hard as getting ready for a prom." Sabrina held the cat at arm's length. "Sorry, but I don't want black cat hair all over my coat."

"Your coat is dark gray," Salem said. "A few black cat hairs will hardly matter."

"I guess." Sabrina set the cat on the fender of the truck and patted the smooth, perfect bun at the nape of her neck. "Do I look okay?"

"Fine." Sabrina looked wonderful in light gray britches and a baby blue shirt and matching choker, but Salem didn't say so. A coach had to stay focused on the important stuff, like winning, so Sabrina would treat him to heaps of exotic victory snacks. "You've only got twenty minutes to warm up before the show starts. Where's George?"

"Over there." Sabrina pointed toward the ring. Carol and Toni were both mounted and walking through the gate. Dixie was holding George while Mike ran a soft rag over his chocolate-colored coat to give it a last-minute shine. When the instructor saw her looking his way, he waved her over. "Well, guess I'd better go."

"I'll be on the rail to give you pointers and moral support." Salem jumped down from the truck as Sabrina hurried off and muttered, "I have a feeling you're going to need it."

Picking a path to avoid horse hooves and boots, Salem darted out of the parking area in a wooded grove, across the open staging area by the gate, and around the top end of the rectangular arena. The show ring was just like the ring at the stable, except it was bigger.

Salem sat on a tall tree stump that gave him a perfect view. It was close enough to the fence so Sabrina could hear him if he needed to fire off instructions when she passed. While he waited for her to mount up and enter the ring, he checked his surroundings for likely sources of edible tidbits. The entire area swarmed with spectators, trainers, and grooms. They would all munch lunches they had brought in coolers and baskets or patronize the snack bar set up near the barns. Although he would have to compete with the local squirrels for the dropped goodies, he was satisfied he wouldn't starve.

"There's Salem!" Hilda's voice rang out.

Salem glanced back to see Hilda and Zelda coming toward him through the trees. They had both dressed casually in slacks, long-sleeve blouses, and sturdy shoes. Hilda carried a video camera, and Zelda wore a wide-brimmed straw hat. As they rushed over to join him, the cat turned his attention back to the gate. Mike was just giving Sabrina a leg up.

"Oh, good. The show hasn't started yet." Clutching her hat to her head with one hand, Zelda glanced around. "Where's Sabrina?"

"Just coming in the gate." Salem cast a curious glance at Zelda from the corner of his eye. "How did Zeke's show biz debut turn out last night?"

Zelda shrugged.

"Well, a disguise can't create talent where none exists," Salem observed dryly. Zelda shot the cat a look.

"But the night wasn't a total loss," Hilda explained. "Zeke's fans passed the hat to send him back to clown college. I made just enough to cover the financial deficit created by all the Zelda cousins."

"Well, I'm glad everyone will soon be back where they belong," Zelda sighed.

"Assuming Sabrina doesn't break anything today," Salem said. He held his paws up to his eyes as Sabrina walked George into the ring. Instead of a relaxed, poised posture, she was hunched over clutching the front of the saddle. Because she was holding onto the short, taut reins for dear life, too, the horse couldn't move his head and neck. "We seem to have a major malfunction."

Hilda held the camera up to her eye to check the focus, then lowered it to watch as George stumbled toward them. "Well, it looks like Sabrina reversed her ability spell."

Salem felt a surge of hope as Sabrina released her hold on the reins a bit. However, when she tried to straighten up, she chickened out and immediately hunched over again.

"Doesn't she look precious in her riding habit?" Zelda smiled. "So prim and proper."

Salem didn't voice his opinion. Although correct attire was required, the judges didn't give points for looking precious. In fact, they wouldn't give Sabrina a second look if she didn't loosen up and act as though she had some clue about riding.

"Okay, ladies, this is an emergency," Salem said as Sabrina steered George toward the fence. Sabrina was so tense, a stiff breeze could have toppled her off the saddle. Fortunately, the air was perfectly still, but he doubted that would make any difference. "Heavy on the positive pep talk, please."

"Hi." Sabrina gave her aunts a slight nod without releasing her death grip on the saddle. "I wish I could say I was glad to see you, but I'm about to make a public spectacle of myself and disgrace the entire Spellman family."

"Don't be so hard on yourself." Hilda set the camera down and grabbed Sabrina's hand. She pried the girl's fingers apart and lengthened the reins so George's chin wasn't touching his chest. "You'll be fine."

"That's what I thought until I actually got on George a couple minutes ago," Sabrina said. "I've forgotten everything I never learned about riding a horse."

"It can't possibly be that bad." Zelda's hat slipped when she tilted her head. Rather than dealing with it, she pointed and the hat disappeared. There were trees so she didn't need to pack her own shade, Salem surmised.

"Worse. I should have told you about the ability spell." Sabrina looked totally despondent. "The only reason I didn't was because I was embarrassed about messing up the wording. So now I'm stuck in a horse show with George and Mike depending on me, and I *still* don't know how to ride!"

"That's the *real* problem with using an ability spell, Sabrina," Zelda said. "You don't realize how much ability you actually do have when you remove it."

Sabrina blinked. "Seriously?"

Salem, Hilda, and Zelda all nodded.

Salem, being the official coach, tried to drive the point home. "It's not just a question of thinking you can, Sabrina. You've got to *know* you can . . . because you can."

Hilda rolled her eyes. "Just go out there and give it your best shot, Sabrina. That's all anyone can expect."

"Right." Zelda raised a determined fist. "It's not whether you win or lose. It's how you play the game. Or, in this case, how you ride the horse."

Sabrina nodded and smiled tightly, but she didn't look convinced. Under the circumstances, Salem wasn't surprised. If she didn't come through, it might take Mike years to save enough money to go to veterinary school, and George would end up working the trail ride shift at Green Hills.

Chapter 10

Mike's tense look faded when Sabrina and George walked out of the woods. After talking to her aunts and Salem, Sabrina had decided she'd have better luck trying to get her riding groove back without an audience. Since Mike had been giving Carol and Toni pointers for their novice equitation class, she hadn't interrupted to tell him she was leaving to warm up on the trails.

"I am so sorry, Mike," Sabrina said when she realized the instructor had been searching for her. She should have known he'd worry if she vanished without notification.

"Well, you're looking a lot more relaxed." Smiling, Mike turned and walked beside the horse back toward the arena. "It's amazing how calming the woods can be, isn't it?"

"'Amazing' doesn't even begin to describe it," Sabrina agreed. Jumping a log on the trails had helped cure her fear of jumping. She had only walked and trotted

George along the bridle path that circled the show grounds, but that had been enough to settle her nerves. That wasn't enough to insure success, but it was a start. Sabrina reached down and patted the horse's neck. "We're both better now."

"I can see that," Mike said as they moved up to the fence near the rest of the class. "Everybody gets horse show jitters before a class, even when they've done it a hundred times."

"I'll remember that." Without thinking, Sabrina looped the buckled reins around her right hand and brushed a wisp of hair under her hat with her left. She continued to let the reins droop so George could relax, too, unaware that she was slipping back into the state of comfortable confidence she had known under the ability spell.

"Good. Green Hunter Hack goes into the ring next." Mike squeezed her booted leg then moved up to the rails to watch the rest of the beginning equitation flat class.

Exhaling to relieve her lingering tension, Sabrina did a quick scan of the grounds. Aunt Hilda was still with Salem. Apparently prompted by the cat, she seemed to be offering encouragement and tips to Carol and Toni as they trotted past.

Cindy, Veronica, and Debra were huddled with Edward on the far side of the staging area. Based on the serious intensity evident on all their faces, the girls were getting last-minute instructions. Johnny and the other two Adams College grooms were walking Goldie, Moon Shadow, and Crazy Quilt nearby.

Aunt Zelda was talking with two men while she waited in line at the refreshment stand. Sabrina thought she recognized the shorter man with brown hair and a dour expression from campus, but she didn't know his name. Sabrina's mouth fell open when Aunt Zelda pointed in her direction and the second man turned to look.

It was Debra's father.

"Thank goodness I had the good sense not to blab about Debra's annoying snobbery to my aunts," Sabrina mumbled. Still, she breathed easier when Zelda moved up to the concession window to order and the two men drifted away. She was fully prepared to take the heat if something went horribly wrong in the hack class, but she really didn't want her aunt hanging out with Debra's dad when it happened.

"Aren't Carol and Toni doing great?" Beth grinned at Sabrina, rocked back on her heels, and popped her gum.

Sabrina glanced into the ring, wishing she had paid closer attention to her friends. There were over thirty riders in Novice Equitation and the competition was intense. However, she was sure that, since they knew the green hunter classes would make it or break it for Mike and George, they would forgive her. Besides, she hadn't missed the whole class.

"Yes!" Sabrina exclaimed when the judges called for the second canter. "They both picked up the right lead."

Beth leaned forward and squinted. "Hey, they did!"

Dixie and Gretchen both crossed their fingers and

jiggled with excitement when Toni cantered by on Cameo.

"Looking good, girl!" Dixie said, being careful not to yell too loudly. It would not be cool to startle the other riders' horses.

Sabrina gave Carol and Pepper a toned-down "Woohoo!"

Although they tried to keep their team spirit dampened to acceptable levels while the class was in progress, Cindy, Veronica, and Debra all turned to gawk. Debra walked away with an I-don't-know-these-people look and yanked Goldie's reins out of Johnny's hand. Veronica and Cindy just mounted up. Nobody else in the beginning equitation group seemed to notice the aloof attitude of the advanced Adams riders. Their total attention was on the horses lining up side by side in the middle of the ring.

Sabrina's stomach knotted as the woman judge walked behind them, jotting or not jotting notes on a clipboard. Was she taking points off or putting them on? On, Sabrina decided when the judge walked passed Toni and Carol without even a glance. She was disappointed but not surprised when Toni and Carol were not among the six ribbon winners.

They were champs as far as Mike and their friends were concerned, though. Even better, Sabrina realized. Judging from Toni and Carol's glowing faces and wide smiles as they left the ring, they had taken Cindy's advice and just had fun.

"That was the most exciting time I have ever had!"

Toni slipped to the ground and threw her arms around Cameo's neck. "You were so good, Cameo. Wasn't she great?"

"The best." Mike gave Toni a quick hug and Carol a thumbs-up. "You were both wonderful."

"I'm still shaking." Carol giggled.

"But your worst fear didn't come to pass, Carol," Beth said. "You stayed on."

"I was too scared to fall off!" Carol swung her leg over the saddle and to the ground. When her legs buckled and she sank into a sitting position, Beth took Pepper's reins and moved him away. "Just call me noodle knees," Carol said, laughing.

A brief moment of screeching feedback from the public address system preceded the next announcement. "All horses for the Green Hunter Hack class please enter the ring now."

Sabrina's throat went dry. She took a deep breath and shortened the reins. George's big moment had finally arrived.

"I *so* wanted Carol and Toni to win something." Dixie stroked George's nose. "I guess it's up to you, Sabrina. The glory of the Adams College Beginning Equitation Class is riding on your shoulders."

"Literally," Beth added.

"Relax and enjoy yourself, Sabrina," Mike said. "A horse show is *not* life and death in a salt mine."

Sabrina nodded, but she knew that statement wasn't entirely true. Not for George. He was ten years old and could live to be twenty-five or older. How he spent those remaining years very much depended on how they performed in the class. *And,* she thought as she walked the horse toward the gate, *since George is an ordinary horse again, his destiny is totally in my hands.*

The responsibility felt like an anchor dragging Sabrina's spirits down as she paused to let several other horses enter the ring ahead of her.

"Are you going in or not?" Debra snapped as she rode up behind George. She didn't wait for an answer. "Oh, never mind. Just stay out of my way during this class, Sabrina. They shouldn't even allow rank beginners to enter and muck things up."

Although Debra's attitude did nothing to elevate her mood, Sabrina was pleasantly surprised when George completely ignored Goldie as she sashayed into the ring. Sabrina didn't know if he had stopped caring or was playing hard to get. Either way, they had a better chance of doing well if he was focused on what he was doing and not on the pretty chestnut mare.

Sabrina was treated to an even bigger surprise when Cindy moved Moon Shadow up beside George.

"Remember, Sabrina. Watch your hat and have a good time." With a wink and a smile, Cindy nudged Shadow into a jog and moved ahead.

In another totally unexpected gesture of goodwill, Veronica touched the brim of her hard hat as she rode Crazy Quilt past George and into the ring behind Shadow.

The genuine displays of camaraderie had a jolting effect on Sabrina, which resulted in an instant attitude adjustment. No matter what happened, she didn't have to be ashamed for trying and doing the best she could.

And neither did George.

Touching the horse's side with her heel, Sabrina rode into the ring at a brisk sitting trot with some of her confidence restored. She didn't know how, but one way or another everything was going to work out okay, even if they placed last in the class of fifteen.

Sabrina slowed George to a walk two horse-lengths behind Crazy Quilt as one of the ring crew people closed the gate. Aunt Zelda was standing with the man from the college and beamed as she rode by.

"You look perfect, Sabrina!" Zelda said. "Just keep your back straight, your elbows in, and your heels down and you'll be fine!"

Her aunt's basic equitation advice made Sabrina smile and helped her relax. Thirty feet farther along the fence, Salem and Aunt Hilda put in their two cents' worth.

"Stay clear of the pack," Salem reminded her. "The judge can't judge a horse she can't see."

"Right! And confidence counts, so smile." Hilda leaned over the fence, still talking as Sabrina moved beyond her. "You have to look like you're having a great time even if you're so terrified you feel like throwing up."

Rather than have *that* inspiring image planted in her mind for the duration of the class, Sabrina eliminated thoughts about everything except George and the announcer's voice. Now that she was actually riding in the show ring, she realized it wasn't much different from riding in the practice arena back at Adams. The biggest plus, however, was that George was behaving like an ideal hunter. Although they were still walking, he moved freely and boldly without the slightest suggestion that he was difficult to handle.

"I know I can. I know I can." Sabrina repeated Salem's mantra several times under her breath. When the announcer asked the class to trot, she reacted automatically.

George eased into the sweeping two-beat gait when she squeezed his sides. Sabrina missed the diagonal on her first try, but sat a double-down within two more strides to correct herself. Since George was the one being judged, she didn't think the slip in equitation would matter. There was no point worrying about something she couldn't change anyway.

George's stride was much longer than that of Veronica's horse. As they trotted around the ring to the left, Sabrina realized George was in danger of getting so close to Crazy Quilt, he might falter. To avoid that, she gently steered him out from the rail a bit, and they trotted past Veronica without incident.

"Walk, please!" The announcer's voice boomed over the P.A.

Sabrina flexed her hands to apply pressure on the reins without actually pulling to bring George back down to a walk. Her palms began to sweat while she walked on, waiting for the announcer to ask for a canter. They were moving to the left, and that was George's bad lead.

Taking a quick, deep breath, Sabrina desperately tried to remember everything she was supposed to do. Although she hadn't been able to watch the other horses in the class closely, she was certain none of them had made a major mistake. If George missed his lead, they wouldn't stand a chance of ending up in the ribbons.

"A little pressure on the reins, nudge with my right heel, shift my weight back and to the right." Already primed when the command came, Sabrina gave George the cue. Since she was positioned correctly, he automatically led off with his left leg. However, since Sabrina was no longer riding with the ability spell, she wasn't quite prepared to cope with the faster, rocking gait.

Her right boot slipped out of her stirrup, and she bounced so hard her backside thumped against the saddle. The only thing that saved her from a disqualifying nosedive into the dirt was her absolute trust in George. He didn't shy to the side or buck in protest. The horse just kept moving, his stride steady and strong.

With her heart in her throat, Sabrina managed to get her foot back in the stirrup. Once she felt secure, she quickly settled into the familiar rhythm. By the time they rounded the far end of the arena where the judge's eye and attention were focused, she was riding as though she knew exactly what she was doing.

Sabrina couldn't help but notice that the lady judge watched George for several long seconds, then made a note on her clipboard. Convinced that this was a good sign, Sabrina finally smiled.

With George's left lead and the worst behind her, Sabrina actually enjoyed riding through the rest of the Green Hunter Hack class. Although she continued to concentrate on George, she was also a little more aware of her support groups on the rail.

Toni and the other girls from the Adams stable raised victorious fists when the Hunter Hack class reversed direction and Sabrina walked past them going to the right.

Mike's dark eyes shone with pride. "Just keep going with the flow, Sabrina. You're doing fine."

When she trotted by Salem and Hilda, her aunt lowered the video camera and asked the cat, "Are you sure Sabrina removed the ability spell? I don't think she'd like being a dull star on the far fringes of the galaxy for the next fifteen years."

Definitely not, Sabrina thought, relieved that she had done the right thing.

Engrossed in conversation with the college guy and Debra's dad, Aunt Zelda just waved and smiled.

Since Mike had warned her the judge might ask for something in addition to the usual walk, trot, and canter routine, Sabrina wasn't thrown off when the announcer asked for a hand-gallop while they were cantering. George lengthened his stride when she shifted forward in the saddle, but he never threatened to race out of control. She even managed to keep him on the rail when several other horses dramatically cut corners and ran closer to the center.

"Walk your horses, on the buckle, please!" the announcer said.

On the buckle? Sabrina glanced around as she brought George back to a walk. Riding near her, Cindy caught her puzzled look and lifted her right hand. The redheaded girl was holding the buckle that connected the left and right reins.

Mouthing a thank-you, Sabrina moved her hand to the buckle. George walked quietly until the class was instructed to line up. No one said a word while the judge walked behind the line, pausing by one horse and moving past the next, taking notes before making her final decision. Everyone tensed when the judge's assistant carried the results to the announcer's stand.

The announcer cleared his throat. "First place for Green Hunter Hack goes to number forty-five, Golden Wings, owned and ridden by Debra Sheridan."

Polite applause and a few cheers rose from the crowd. Sabrina thought she heard Debra's father say, "That's my daughter."

The red, second-place ribbon was awarded to a horse and rider Sabrina didn't know. Cindy's horse, Moon Shadow, won third.

"Way, Cindy!" Sabrina grinned as the girl rode over to the ring steward to collect her prize.

Veronica dropped her reins to applaud. When Sabrina caught her eye, they both crossed their fingers, each wishing the other good luck.

"Fourth place goes to number thirty-six, Mission Impossible," the announcer said. "Owned by John Adams College and ridden by Sabrina Spellman."

"Yes!" Aunt Hilda yelled.

Stunned, Sabrina walked George toward the steward in a daze. Murmuring a quiet "thank-you," she took her white, gold-embossed ribbon and jogged out the gate.

"The school owns that number thirty-six horse, Mr. Flanagan?" Debra's father asked Aunt Zelda's acquaintance from the college.

"Apparently so, Robert." The man gave Sabrina a stiff smile as she rode past. "What was his name?"

"Mission Impossible," Aunt Zelda answered, "but he'd rather be called George."

"You're sure of that?" Robert Sheridan asked, thinking she was joking.

"Positive," Zelda said.

Momentarily trapped in the jam of horses around the gate, Sabrina waved her ribbon and grinned at Mike and her friends, who were still gathered by the rail several feet away. Off to her left, she saw Veronica exit the ring with a green sixth-place ribbon. The tall, thin girl rode over to join Cindy and Edward under a shade tree. Any pride Veronica felt about placing sixth out of fifteen evaporated when Edward frowned.

"What's the matter with you today, Veronica?" Edward asked coldly. "How could you let a common school horse beat a fine thoroughbred like Moon Shadow?"

Sabrina's high spirits dipped suddenly. Even though George had just won a fourth-place ribbon, Edward still regarded him as a common lesson horse!

"Don't let that ribbon go to your head, Sabrina." Debra handed Goldie's reins to Johnny and eyed Sabrina with unconcealed contempt as the groom led the mare away. "That was just the hack class. There's no way Impossible Mission—"

"Mission Impossible," Sabrina corrected her curtly.

"Whatever," Debra said with marked intolerance. "I just hate to see you embarrass yourself trying to prove that horse is a hunter when he's not. I mean, you'll both be out of your league in the over fences class, so why bother? Just trying to help."

Sure you are, Sabrina thought as Debra shrugged and left to join her father. The problem was that Debra might be right.

Sabrina couldn't deny that the ability spell had created a false sense of security and she had not really overcome her fear of jumping. Trusting George to take care of her didn't work anymore, either, now that he was just an ordinary horse again. And she couldn't overlook the fact that the jumps set up in the show ring were a lot higher than logs in the woods.

All of that was pretty intimidating, but her problems didn't end there. Sabrina fought a surge of panic when the announcer's voice blared from the speakers. The horses in the Green Hunter Over Fences class were being called to assemble by the gate, and she didn't know the course!

Chapter 11

Sabrina stood beside Mike at the rail, watching the first horse and rider complete the Green Hunter jump course. Things had been happening so fast since the end of the Green Hunter Hack class, she was having trouble staying focused.

After everyone had congratulated her and made a fuss over George, Sabrina had given the white, fourth-place ribbon to Aunt Zelda to hold. Mr. Flanagan, who was on the John Adams College Board of Regents, seemed very impressed, but she hadn't had time to stay and chat. Robert Sheridan had left to be with Debra and Edward. Hilda and Salem were sharing an order of fries at a picnic table while they waited for Sabrina's turn. Since Sabrina would be fifth to ride, Dixie had taken George to get a quick drink so she could memorize the order of the jumps.

"You'll have to be careful on that far line," Mike warned.

"Line? What line?" Sabrina checked the printed course diagram Mike had given her. The word "line" wasn't on the paper.

"The two fences that are on the far side of the ring," Cindy said. "That's called a line."

Mike and Sabrina both glanced back to see Cindy and Veronica behind them. They were both mounted and, apparently, listening to Mike with great interest.

"Those two fences are closer together than the other jumps in the course," Veronica added. "So it's harder."

"Oh." Sabrina blinked.

"Good job in the Green Hunter Hack class," Mike told the newcomers. "You both rode well. Edward must be very proud."

"Yeah." Toni gave the mounted girls one of her snappy salutes. Beth and Gretchen were astride Cameo and Pepper, walking the horses near the ring so they could watch the class. Carol had rushed to the rest room, leaving Toni to boost Sabrina's morale. "Adams College won four out of six ribbons. Not bad at all."

"Not according to Edward," Veronica said.

Cindy sighed. "By his definition, Veronica and I *lost* because we placed third and sixth instead of second and third."

Mike hesitated, obviously disturbed. "Aside from the fact that being a good sport and doing your best are just as important as winning, nobody can win *all* the time."

"I wish." Cindy's eyes snapped to the right. Everyone followed her gaze. Edward was talking with Debra by the gate, giving her some last-minute advice. She was next to ride. "Debra always wins."

"At least, it seems that way." Veronica shrugged.

"Uh-huh. Well—" Mike turned back to Sabrina and pointed across the ring. "That far line can be taken in five or six strides. Since George has a long stride and likes to move at a good clip, you'd better go for a forward five. He might chip in if you try holding him down to six strides."

"Chip in?" Sabrina's voice cracked with nervousness.

"That means the horse is too close to the jump when he leaves the ground," Cindy explained.

"You want me to *count* the strides between the jumps?" Sabrina looked at Mike, aghast. "I'll be lucky to remember the course and get around without falling off!"

"It doesn't seem to matter if I try for five strides or six." Cindy sighed. "Moon Shadow always seems to be half a stride off."

"I've noticed that when you practice," Mike said. "Shadow has a shorter than normal stride, Cindy. He can't cover enough ground in five strides or six if you hold him in check. I don't know what Edward's told you, but if it were up to me, I'd do that short line in a driving six."

Cindy frowned, thinking. "I bet that will work. Edward always wants five because he says judges usually like a horse that moves big."

"Some do, I guess," Mike agreed. "But *all* hunter judges like a horse that moves and jumps smoothly and consistently."

"Got any words of wisdom about Crazy Quilt?" Veronica asked.

"Let her move on a little." Mike shrugged self-consciously. "You're a good rider, Veronica. You don't have to go slow to stay on."

"So *that's* why you guys are here," Toni teased. "Trying to pick Mike's brains, huh?"

"Well, we won't turn down sound advice," Cindy said.

"Especially if it'll help us beat *Debra*." Veronica put an emphasis on the name, suggesting she didn't appreciate Debra's arrogant attitude.

Cindy shifted in her saddle, looking a bit awkward. "Edward's a terrific trainer, I guess, but—"

Veronica wasn't shy. "He pays a lot more attention to Debra because her father donates big bucks to the college."

"Advice isn't the only reason we came over, though," Cindy added. "The truth is that you guys are having a lot more fun."

"You don't mind, do you?" Veronica asked cautiously.

"Nope." Toni laughed and draped an arm over Carol's shoulders as she rejoined the group. "Mike Santori's Traveling Horse and Pony Show is always open to honest party crashers. The more the merrier. Right, Carol?"

"Works for me," Carol said.

"I hear you. We all go to Adams so we *should* hang together." Sabrina was glad that Cindy and Veronica had gotten into the team spirit, but that wouldn't help her get through the jumping class. The second contestant had just finished and Debra was entering the ring. It was almost Sabrina's turn and she still wasn't sure of the course.

"Here comes Dixie with George," Mike said. "Let's watch Debra's round and then you can mount up."

Sabrina nodded, her gaze glued to Golden Wings. Although she didn't care for Debra's annoying personality, the girl was an experienced and accomplished rider. If she was going to take her cues from someone, Debra was the best choice.

"George!" Dixie pulled on the reins and dug in her heels to stop the horse, but George seemed determined to get closer to Sabrina. Dixie stopped fighting him when she realized she couldn't win.

"Hi, George." Sabrina smiled when the horse moved up beside her. As Debra circled Goldie to start her round, Sabrina was tempted to cast another talking spell so George could ease her mind about their upcoming trial. She didn't because she wasn't a cheater. Instead, she absently rubbed the horse's chin and studied Debra.

Even George seemed to be paying strict attention to Goldie's every move. A whicker rumbled in his throat as the chestnut mare jumped the first freshly painted fence opposite their position on the rail.

Sabrina wasn't experienced enough to be sure, but as Debra guided Goldie around the course it certainly looked as though they were performing flawlessly.

"Doesn't she ever make a mistake?" Veronica sighed as Debra and Goldie sailed over the final fence.

"I don't know if the judge caught it, but Goldie was off a little on those first two fences." Mike shrugged, indicating the two jumps on their side of the ring.

George curled his lip back.

"George! Did you deliberately distract Debra's horse?" Sabrina eyed the mischievous gelding with a stern expression.

Everyone laughed when George shook his head "yes."

"Okay, that does it." Carol threw up her hands. "Now I *know* George understands everything you say, Sabrina."

I wish, Sabrina thought, putting on her helmet and fastening the chin strap. When she moved to George's left side and bent her knee for a leg up, the horse nuzzled her arm and whickered again as though he was trying to reassure her. Sabrina looked the horse in the eye, wondering if he could possibly remember everything they had been through the past two weeks. The next thing she knew, Dixie had grabbed her bent leg and hoisted her into the saddle. As Mike led George to the staging area by the gate, she accepted the fact that the moment of recognition had been nothing more than her imagination.

Wishful thinking wouldn't make George into something more than a normal horse, Sabrina reminded herself. Only magic could do that. However, George didn't need magic to be all that he could be based on his natural abilities.

All he needed was her.

"Just talk George around the course, Sabrina, and you'll have it made," Carol said.

"Whatever works," Veronica said. "I'd carry American flags and sing the 'Star Spangled Banner' if that would help Crazy Quilt get around."

"Remember, take five strides on the far line." Mike spoke to Sabrina without taking his eye off the current contestant. He winced when the girl's horse knocked the top rail off the flower-box jump.

Sabrina nodded, but the voices around her were just background noise as she watched the fourth rider and cemented the order of the jumps in her mind. George, Mike, and everyone in her equitation class were depending on her, and she wasn't going to let them down.

"Okay, Sabrina. You're on." Mike smiled and squeezed her booted leg as the fourth rider exited the ring.

"Here goes nothing." Sabrina patted George's neck and picked up her reins.

"Just do your best." Mike held Sabrina's gaze for a second, his eyes brimming with pride and affection. He broke the connection suddenly and pointed through the gate. "Go!"

Taking a deep breath, Sabrina walked George into the ring and along the fence. She smiled with a curt nod at Aunt Zelda and Mr. Flanagan.

"Just relax," Zelda said, clasping her hands. "Pretend you're puddle jumping through the ice fields on Europa."

"Puddle jumping on one of Jupiter's moons?" Mr.

Flanagan's austere expression vanished when he laughed. "Oh, you *are* a delight, Ms. Spellman. Most academics are so insufferably stuffy."

Sabrina walked on a few more feet. She didn't want to ignore Salem and Hilda before she changed directions to circle.

"Just remember one thing," the cat said, apparently unaware that he had an unsightly dab of red ketchup stuck to the black hair on his chin. "George can do it."

"You have ketchup on your chin," Hilda told Salem. He licked a paw. Hilda lifted her video camera to her eye and started taping. "Just ride, Sabrina. How hard can it be?"

"No harder than jumping logs in the woods," Sabrina muttered as she steered George toward the center of the ring. "And we're starting out on your good lead, George. Get ready."

With Aunt Hilda's advice fresh in her mind, Sabrina cued the horse into a controlled canter moving to the right. Sitting easy in the saddle, she steered George over to the rail, back along the end of the ring past her aunts and the gate, and toward the first line.

Mike and the equitation class were on the rail by the first of two fences. The two-foot, six-inch-high post and rail jumps were composed of three striped, horizontal rails spaced eight inches apart. The ends of the rails rested on cups attached to a standard or jump support on each side.

"These first two are easy, boy," Sabrina said. Although George didn't understand her, the familiar practice of talking to him kept her hands and her nerves steady.

Riding on instinct, she was aware of every nuance in George's manner and movement. He was primed, and when he left the ground to jump the first fence, she automatically moved forward with him. They landed smoothly, and Sabrina found herself automatically counting off the strides between fences. On the count of eight, George sailed over the second fence.

Sabrina felt like she was flying. Flush with excitement and tension, she had to remind herself not to get too cocky. They still had six fences to go.

"That was perfect, George." Putting the tiniest tad of pressure on the reins, Sabrina gently checked George's speed as they cantered along the far end of the ring. When they started down the far side, Sabrina turned George toward the next two fences, which were set on a diagonal across the ring.

The line consisted of another vertical post and rail followed by a gate. The second fence wasn't as solid as it looked. The jump had been designed so the two white, side-by-side panels topped with two striped rails were not permanently fastened to the standards. If a horse hit the fence, the rails and panels would fall easily so no one would be hurt.

Holding a steady rhythm, George leaped both fences without chipping in or jumping too big.

Sabrina put a lid on her elation as they came off the gate. The real test of George's hunter potential was still ahead. As Sabrina rode toward the corner of the ring, she had to shift George onto his bad lead before they reached the fence and turned left. Putting pressure on the reins and shifting her weight, she cued the horse to change.

George altered his stride so he was leading with his left front leg, but something was wrong. He wasn't cantering with the same gentle rocking-horse gait he usually had.

"He missed the back lead!" Aunt Hilda waved anxiously as Sabrina rode by.

Uh-oh. Sabrina understood instantly. George had switched leads on his front legs but not his back, something a more experienced rider might have figured out and corrected before they were heading for the line with the short distance between jumps.

Trying not to let the unnerving situation get the best of her, Sabrina gently tugged the right rein and nudged George in the right side. She felt the slight bump in his stride when he made the correction, but the fluctuation threw her concentration off. She wasn't quite ready when George launched himself over the first fence in the short line. Instead of moving forward with the horse, she was left back slightly, which threw George's balance off a little. He hit a rail with a back hoof, but the rail didn't fall.

Sabrina didn't have time to fret about the mistake as they headed for the second fence in the short line, which was fashioned from two sets of jump standards. The top rail on the first set of standards was set at two feet high. The top rail on the second set of standards was set at two feet, six inches. The space between the two top rails was about eighteen inches. Remembering Mike's advice, Sabrina let George extend himself and move on as she counted off five strides. He jumped over without a problem.

"Good going, George. We're almost there." Sabrina kept a level head as they cantered along the far end of the ring again. She knew the judge would count off for the missed back lead and the rubbed rail, but they were not down and out yet. If Mike was right about Debra, all the riders who had already gone had made mistakes.

"Let's finish this in style, George, and show these people what a school horse can do." Sabrina thought she heard George snort as she checked his speed to turn toward the last diagonal line.

Since George was already on the right lead and the hardest jumps were behind them, Sabrina let herself relax. The last two jumps, a flower box and a simple post and rail, were spaced for eight strides. The flower-box jump was more solid than the gate, but not as high. A top rail was placed over the two narrow planters filled with fake flowers, making it look more intimidating than it was.

Moving with the same steady rhythm he had maintained for the whole class, George jumped the flower box and the final post and rail perfectly.

The instant the horse touched down, Sabrina felt a rush of sheer joy. Ecstatic, but remembering Salem's admonitions about proper horse show etiquette, she suppressed her enthusiasm as she cantered George into a sweeping turn, brought him down to a walk, and sedately left the ring.

For the moment, she wasn't worried about whether they'd place in the ribbons or not. She had made it over all the jumps without going off course or falling off, and George had behaved like a gentleman and a show-class hunter.

In her book, that made them both winners.

Everyone in her cheering section seemed to agree. As soon as George emerged from the equine congestion by the gate, Sabrina's friends from the stable mobbed them. Cindy and Veronica, who weren't riding until the end of the class, made Vs with their fingers for victory. Toni, Carol, and Dixie gushed with congratulations. Beth and Gretchen, who were still mounted on Cameo and Pepper, waved.

Mike motioned for Sabrina to lean down, as though he wanted to whisper in her ear. Instead, he kissed her on the cheek. "You were wonderful, Sabrina."

"Thanks, Mike." Sabrina blushed. "We couldn't have done it without you."

"I promised Cindy and Veronica I'd help them through this class," Mike said, giving George a pat and her hand a squeeze. "But maybe you and I can get together later."

Sabrina smiled, hoping he couldn't tell that her heart had just lurched and started pounding madly. "What should I do now?"

"Ride around, relax, whatever you want." Mike cocked an eyebrow in playful warning. "Just don't wander too far away. The class will probably last another hour or so. They'll announce the winners shortly after the last horse goes."

As Sabrina's adrenaline rush subsided, she was seized by a mental tiredness that sometimes follows immense relief. Needing to unwind before she dealt with her aunts' energetic exuberance, she slipped off George and loosened the girth. After taking the horse back to the van for a drink, she found a grassy spot in the shade where George could graze while she watched the rest of the class.

Now that she knew what it was like to ride over fences, Sabrina could relate to everything the other riders encountered. Her stomach tightened when a horse refused or knocked down a rail, and her chest swelled when someone finished without anything serious going wrong. As far as she could tell, Cindy and Moon Shadow completed the course without making a single mistake. Crazy Quilt rubbed a rail that almost fell, but other than that, Veronica did well, too.

When the last horse entered the ring, Sabrina tightened George's girth, found a stump, and mounted again. Salem and Aunt Hilda were standing near the gate when she arrived to await the results of the class.

"I never realized horse shows could be so exciting." Aunt Hilda's video camera was packed in her shoulder bag. She cradled Salem in her arms.

Spotting Cindy and Veronica, Sabrina excused herself and rode George over to join them. "You guys have done this so often, you're probably not tense with anticipation—are you?"

"Spring coiled." Cindy shrugged apologetically. "The whole point of entering a show is to win."

"You absolutely have to be a good sport no matter what," Veronica said, "but it's a lot more fun to be a good winner than a good loser."

Sabrina nodded, determined to hide her disappointment if she and George didn't win anything. However, it was refreshing to hear someone admit that they preferred to win. At least, Cindy and Veronica were honest.

"And now the results of Green Hunter Over Fences," the announcer said. "First place goes to number forty, Moon Shadow, owned and ridden by Cynthia Webber."

"Me?" Cindy squealed. "Ohmigod!"

"Woohoo!" Veronica patted Cindy on the back.

"What?" Debra's voice rang out above the crowd. "That's got to be a mistake!"

"Better get in there and collect your blue ribbon before Debra convinces the judge she was wrong." Sabrina waved Cindy toward the ring and glanced back as the announcer called the second-place winner. She located Debra just as the girl realized she hadn't won the red ribbon, either. Debra's face darkened with petulance.

Robert Sheridan was standing with Edward and another man in boots and britches Sabrina didn't know. He stepped toward Debra, scowling.

"And in third," the announcer said, "number forty-five, Golden Wings, owned and ridden by Debra Sheridan."

"Third?" Debra's eyes flashed as her temper flared. "That's an insult! I can't believe—"

"Shut up and go get your ribbon, Debra." Mr. Sheridan glared at his stunned daughter.

Debra didn't argue. As she walked Goldie toward the ring, Edward pointed at Sabrina and George. The other man turned to look and nodded.

"Do you know that guy, Veronica?" Sabrina asked. "The one Edward's talking to?"

Veronica looked back and wrinkled her nose. "That's Hank Stanley. He owns that rental stable, Green Hills."

Sabrina stared, numb with disbelief. There could be only one reason why the two men were so interested in George. Edward was trying to sell him to Mr. Stanley as a rental horse.

When the announcer called George's number for fifth place, Sabrina was too bummed to care.

Chapter 12

Driving back to the college stables, Sabrina glanced at the white fourth-place ribbon and pink fifth-place ribbon lying on the dashboard, wondering why people thought they were so important. Although the college owned George, Mr. Flanagan had insisted that she keep the prizes. They would look great in that blank space on her bulletin board, but they weren't worth a horse's life.

Unfortunately, it seemed that Edward didn't think fourth and fifth places were good enough to qualify George as a real show hunter.

Everything had been so hectic after the Green Hunter Hack Over Fences class ended, Sabrina hadn't had an opportunity to actually ask Edward about his plans for George. However, there was no doubt that the head instructor had threatened to get rid of George two weeks ago. She was assuming the worst since Edward and Mr. Stanley from the Green Hills Rental Stable had been discussing the horse with such intense interest.

The fact that Edward had never spoken to her or ac-knowledged her existence didn't make the prospect of a rational discussion likely, but Sabrina was determined to break the ice before George got shipped out.

Even if I have to use a little magic to get Edward's attention, Sabrina thought as she turned into the college stable drive. She had stayed behind the slower, six-horse van just in case the driver had detoured to Green Hills to drop off George. George was still on the van, but everyone else had beaten them back to the barn.

Mike had ridden with Dixie and Gretchen in Johnny's extended cab truck, which was parked be-tween her aunts' car and Mr. Sheridan's large SUV. Ed-ward wasn't back yet, since his car was not in its usual spot.

"We're here!" Sabrina glanced into the backseat. Toni and Carol jerked awake and rubbed their eyes.

"I can't believe I fell asleep." Carol stretched and rubbed her neck.

"A horse show is a lot more tiring than I thought it would be." Toni yawned. "Mostly because of all the work you have to do before and after."

Beth sighed from the passenger seat. "I'm sorry it's over, and even sorrier I didn't try to compete."

"Maybe there will be a next time, Beth," Sabrina said as she parked and turned off the engine. "Just sign up for the Intermediate Equitation class."

"Great idea!" Brightening, Beth hopped out and ran toward the van with Toni and Carol on her heels.

Sabrina hung back, dragging her feet in the dirt as

she trudged down the drive. George wouldn't be moving out today, but she dreaded having to tell him that their plan had failed. He had tried so hard and accomplished so much, she was afraid his heart would break. Hers was definitely feeling the strain.

"Hey, Sabrina!" Veronica waved as she led Crazy Quilt around the front of the van. The ramp was on the far side, out of Sabrina's sight.

Veronica had won sixth place in the over fences class, too, and both her green ribbons were clipped to her front pockets. They fluttered as she jogged her horse toward the main barn behind Cindy and Moon Shadow. One of the grooms followed with Goldie.

Through the school barn door, Sabrina could see Dixie, Gretchen, and Beth getting the stalls ready for the returning lesson horses. Beth measured sweet feed and oats into buckets while Dixie filled the water pails. Gretchen hauled a bale of hay into the aisle and pulled off the orange twine that held the flakes together. When Toni and Carol led Cameo and Pepper around the back of the van, Sabrina could tell they were glad to be home.

Sabrina quickened her pace with her eye on the back of the truck. She expected to intercept Johnny or the other groom taking George toward the school barn. When no one emerged leading the big liver chestnut horse, she was certain something bad had happened.

Breathless with anxiety, Sabrina dashed around the end of the van and up the ramp. All six stalls inside the truck were empty.

Where is George? Sabrina wondered, her pulse racing. She hadn't taken her eyes off the van since it left the horse show grounds with George on board. She hadn't used a spell to make him vanish, and her aunts wouldn't magically kidnap a horse that wasn't theirs. Distressed, she ran back down the ramp and away from the truck, scanning the whole area. She slouched with relief when she saw Johnny leading George toward the main barn.

"Hey, Johnny! What are you doing?" Sabrina yelled as she broke into a run.

Johnny stopped suddenly. Startled, George jerked his head just as Mike and Mr. Sheridan walked out the stable door. Sabrina slowed to a walk so George wouldn't get more upset.

"Easy does it, boy," Mr. Sheridan said softly, reaching out. The horse calmed down immediately and dropped his muzzle into the man's hand. Mr. Sheridan grinned at Mike. "Look at that!"

Mike nodded. "George has got a lot of sense for a horse, Mr. Sheridan."

"What's going on?" Sabrina asked Mike.

"It looks like George has found a new home," Mike said, smiling.

"I knew it!" Sabrina balled her hands into fists at her sides. She was so angry, she knew she might lose control and throw a magical tantrum. There was no way she'd be able to explain blasting the roof off the barn with a flick of her finger. "How can you look so happy about Edward selling George down the river to Green Hills, Mike?"

"What?" Cindy exclaimed from the shadows just inside the door. She stepped outside, frowning as she munched a sandwich.

"Green Hills?" Mike looked surprised. "George isn't going to Green Hills. Edward is."

"Huh?" Sabrina blinked, totally mystified.

"I know. I couldn't believe it, either." Folding his arms, Mike glanced around the stable grounds, sighed with satisfaction, and smiled. "Apparently, Hank Stanley wants to get into the show horse business to upgrade Green Hills's image. He made Edward an offer Edward couldn't refuse."

"So as of right now, Mike is the new head instructor of the John Adams College riding program." Mr. Sheridan clamped a congratulatory hand on Mike's shoulder.

"That is so great, Mike!" Sabrina was thrilled for him. He deserved the job and the higher pay that went with it. "But why were Edward and Mr. Stanley so interested in George?"

Mr. Sheridan rolled his eyes. "Because Edward told Hank Stanley that *he* had changed George from a lesson horse into a winning show horse."

"What a liar!" Sabrina frowned, incensed at Edward's audacity. However, since Edward was gone and Mike was now in charge of Adams College Stables, the deception had served a good purpose. "So what's happening with George?"

"He's going to Mr. Sheridan's home up north." Mike's grin widened. "Until next year."

"I've been looking for a safe, sound hunter for my

other daughter," Mr. Sheridan explained, noting Sabrina's bewildered expression. "Sandy is a year younger than Debra but not quite as daring. George is the perfect horse for her."

"It's the perfect situation for George, too," Mike said. "He'll be spending the summer on the Sheridan farm, then coming back here with Goldie when Sandy enters Adams as a freshman next year."

"You don't have to worry about George anymore, Sabrina." Mr. Sheridan stroked George's nose, then motioned Johnny to take him into the barn. "Sandy will adore him, and I *never* sell a family horse. They retire out to pasture on our farm. I've had my old mare, Katie Pack, for almost thirty years, since she was five."

Sabrina was so relieved and happy for George, she couldn't speak for a moment.

"Hey!" Cindy yelped, then laughed when George snatched the sandwich out of her hand as he walked by. "I didn't know horses liked peanut butter and jelly."

Mr. Sheridan laughed, too, amused by George's antics.

Good thing, Sabrina thought, since George hadn't lost his mischievous streak when she removed the talking spell.

"I once knew a horse that liked potato chips, onion dip, and soda pop," Aunt Hilda said as she came out of the stable, still holding Salem. Mr. Flanagan and Aunt Zelda were right behind her.

"I've never toured the stables before, Mike." Mr. Flanagan nodded with approval as he looked around. "Very impressive. I think our Adams College riding students should be entering more horse shows, don't you?"

"Absolutely," Mike agreed.

Aunt Zelda cast a sparkling smile at the board member. "Mr. Flanagan has asked Johnny and the other grooms to finish up the chores in both barns so everyone can come to Hilda's Coffeehouse for a victory celebration."

"I've already called ahead," Hilda said. "Josh and Roxie are setting up a buffet."

"I'm buying," Mr. Flanagan added.

"I'll split the cost with you," Mr. Sheridan volunteered. "But Debra can't leave until she finishes taking care of Goldie and cleaning her tack. I don't know where she got the idea that she didn't have to do her own chores, but the vacation's over."

"Would you mind if she had some help, Mr. Sheridan?" Sabrina asked. She didn't know if it was possible to make friends with Debra, but she had to try. Now that Cindy and Veronica had warmed up, she was willing to bet Debra wasn't a lost cause, either. "It *is* a special occasion."

"I'll pitch in so we can get out of here sooner," Cindy said. "Since George ate my sandwich, I'm still famished."

Mr. Sheridan grinned. "I think that would be great."

"Zelda and I will go on ahead to make sure everything's ready," Hilda said. "Besides, we have to take the cat home on our way."

"Wha-mmmmppfff." Salem struggled when Hilda tightened her hold and muffled him.

"I'll take him, Aunt Hilda." Sabrina held out her hands. Salem had been a good equitation coach for her *and* George. It wouldn't be fair to leave him out of the victory party. "I'm sure he wants to say good-bye to George."

Hilda hesitated, reluctant to relinquish the cat because she knew Sabrina was a pushover when he begged.

"Give her the cat, Hilda," Aunt Zelda said firmly. "He's earned one more trip in Sabrina's *saddlebags*."

"Oh, all right!" Hilda handed Salem to Sabrina. "But no food until everyone else leaves."

"Let's hurry up and blow this popstand," Salem said as Sabrina rushed him into the barn. "There's a dozen doughnuts with my name on them."

"You can stop talking or *I'll* take you home before I go to the coffeehouse," Sabrina said. Veronica, Debra, and the grooms all gave her a quizzical look as she rushed by, checking each stall. Johnny had put George across the aisle from Goldie.

Slipping inside, Sabrina pulled the stall door closed. She put Salem in the feed bin and pulled George's head into the corner so they couldn't be seen. Although she was taking a risk, she just had to know if George was happy about how things turned out.

One last time, no joke, no spin,
Make George a chatterbox again.

George's ears perked forward when Sabrina flicked her finger. "Sabrin-mmmmpphhhh!"

"Shhhh!" Sabrina threw her arms around George's head and pressed his face against her chest to muffle him. "Quietly, please!"

"Sorry," George whispered. "I'm just so glad to see you, Sabrina. There's so much to tell."

"I missed being able to talk to you, too." Sabrina eased George's head up and smoothed the long hair of his forelock.

"We sure showed them at the horse show, didn't we?" George chuckled. "We won *two* ribbons!"

"We sure did," Sabrina said. "You probably already know that you're not getting sold to Green Hills."

"Yeah. Woohoo!" George curled his lip back in a grin.

"But how do you feel about going to live with the Sheridans?" Sabrina asked. "Honestly."

"According to Goldie, Sandy is a great kid," George said with enthusiasm. "Kind of quiet and a little shy, but a very caring person. Goldie is absolutely positive that Sandy will love me, and I'll take good care of her. Just like I did you."

"I know you will. That's why Mr. Sheridan likes you so much." Sabrina cleared a lump out of her throat. She was going to miss George a lot more than she had realized. "I guess you're excited because you'll be living so close to Goldie now. Apparently, she's decided to talk to you, too."

"Yeah." George sighed. "I couldn't get her to stop talking on the ride home from the show. She wanted to tell me all about the farm and the other horses there. I have to say, it all sounds like a dream come true."

"I'm sure it is." Smiling, Sabrina hugged the horse's head. "I've got to take the speech spell off again now, George. Have a wonderful life and don't forget me, okay?"

"I won't, Sabrina," George promised solemnly. "Never."

Nodding, Sabrina wiped a tear from her eye and pointed. She wanted to believe that George would cherish the memory of her as much as she'd treasure the memory of him, but with the talking spell gone, that just didn't seem likely.

"Can we go now?" Salem sniffled. "Apparently, I've developed hay fever. It's making my eyes water."

"Sure it is," Sabrina scoffed. "Why don't you just admit you hate to see George go because you really like him?"

"Because the universal rules of feline deportment say we *have* to act indifferent." Salem sighed as Sabrina picked him up and nestled him under her arm. "One misguided display of affection can *totally* destroy a cat's image."

As Sabrina backed out of George's stall for the last time, she blew him a kiss.

George whickered and winked.

About the Author

Diana G. Gallagher lives in Florida with her husband, Marty Burke; four dogs; four cats; and a cranky parrot.

Diana has written more than forty novels for Pocket Books in several series for all age groups, including Star Trek for middle readers, *Sabrina The Teenage Witch, Charmed, Buffy The Vampire Slayer, The Secret World of Alex Mack, Are You Afraid of the Dark,* and *Salem's Tails.*

Gaze into the future and see what wonders lie in store for
Sabrina, The teenage Witch

#40 Dream Boat

Sabrina's newest beau, Christoval Sanchez invites her to
join him on a Spring Break cruise in his native Puerto
Vallarta. But the trip turns out to be anything but
relaxing when Christoval is kidnapped by troll-like
creatures.

Sabrina learns, with the help of her aunts, that christoval
is descended from the Other Realm and has magical
powers that will free his land from an evil spell. Now it's
up to Sabrina to rescue Christoval from the cursed
slumber with an enchanted kiss!

Don't miss out on any of Sabrina's magical antics — conjure
up a book from the past for a truly spellbinding read . . .

#38 Milady's Dragon

Sabrina's roommates Morgan, Miles, and Roxie are
driving her nuts, customers at the coffee shop treat
Sabrina with no respect, and the people at the
drive-through don't smile or say thank you. It seems to
Sabrina that no one has any manners or
sense of humour anymore.

Strolling at a local Medieval Faire, Sabrina loves the
experience. If only she had been born in a time of such
chivalry! In the blink of a witch's eyelash, Sabrina lands
with a thump right in the Middle Ages. The woods are
chock full of noble knights, and even a
fire-breathing dragon. Too bad the natives
don't like witches!

Nancy Drew™

Nancy Drew — Carolyn Keene — Runaway Bride

Nancy Drew — Carolyn Keene — False Pretenses

Nancy Drew — Carolyn Keene — Out of Bounds

Nancy Drew — Carolyn Keene — Making Waves

Nancy Drew — Carolyn Keene — Illusions of Evil

Nancy Drew — Carolyn Keene — Flirting with Danger

Nancy Drew — Carolyn Keene — Fatal Attraction

Nancy Drew — Carolyn Keene — Till Death Do Us Part

DROP DEAD